Browdean Farm & Other Stories by AM Burrage

Alfred McLelland Burrage was born in Hillingdon, Middlesex on 1st July, 1889. His father and uncle were both writers, primarily of boy's fiction, and by age 16 AM Burrage had joined them. The young man had ambitions to write for the adult market too. The money was better and so was his writing.

From 1890 to 1914, prior to the mainstream appeal of cinema and radio the printed word, mainly in magazines, was the foremost mass entertainment. AM Burrage quickly became a master of the market publishing his stories regularly across a number of publications.

By the start of the Great War Burrage was well established but in 1916 he was conscripted to fight on the Western Front. He continued to write during these years documenting his experiences in the classic book War is War by Ex-Private X.

For the remainder of his life Burrage was rarely printed in book form but continued to write and be published on a prodigious scale in magazines and newspapers. In this volume we concentrate on his supernatural stories which are, by common consent, some of the best ever written. Succinct yet full of character each reveals a twist and a flavour that is unsettling.....sometimes menacing....always disturbing.

There are many other volumes available in this series together with a number of audiobooks. All are available from iTunes, Amazon and other fine digital stores.

Table Of Contents

Browdean Farm

Most people with limited vocabularies such as mine would describe the house loosely and comprehensively as picturesque. But it was more than beautiful in its venerable age. It had certain subtle qualities which are called Atmosphere. It invited you, as you approached it along the rough and narrow road which is ignored by those maps which are sold for the use of motorists.

In the language of very old houses it said plainly, 'Come in. Come in.'

It said 'Come in' to Rudge Jefferson and me. In one of the front windows there was a notice, inscribed in an illiterate hand, to the effect that the house was to be let, and that the keys were to be obtained at the first cottage down the road. We went and got them. The woman who handed them over to us remarked that plenty of people looked over the house but nobody ever took it. It had been empty for years.

'Damp and falling to pieces, I suppose,' said Rudge as we returned.

'There's always a snag about these old places.'

The house—Browdean Farm it was called—stood some thirty yards back from the road, at the end of a strip of garden not much wider than its facade. Most of the building was plainly Tudor, but part of it was even earlier. Time was when it had been the property of prosperous yeomen, but now its acres had been added to those of another farm, and it stood shorn of all its land save the small untended gardens in front and behind, and half an acre of apple orchard.

As in most houses of that description the kitchen was the largest room. It was long and lofty and its arched roof was supported by mighty beams which stretched across its breadth. There was a huge range with a noble oven. One could fancy, in the old days of plenty, a score of harvesters supping there after their work, and beer and cider flowing as freely as spring brooks.

To our surprise the place showed few signs of damp, considering the length of time it had been untenanted, and it needed little in the way of repairs. There was not a stick of furniture in the house, but we could tell that its last occupants had been people of refinement and taste. The wallpapers upstairs, the colours of the faded paints and distempers, the presence of a bathroom—that great rarity in old farmhouses—all pointed to the probability of its having been last in the hands of an amateur of country cottages.

Jefferson told me that he knew in his bones—and for once I agreed with his bones—that Nina would love the farm. He was engaged to my sister, and they were waiting until he had saved sufficient money to give them a reasonable material start in matrimony. Like most painstaking writers of no particular reputation Jefferson had to take care of the pence and shillings, but like Nina's, his tastes were inexpensive, and it was an understood thing that they were to live quietly together in the country.

We inquired about the rent. It was astonishingly low. Jefferson had to live somewhere while he finished a book, and he was already paying storage for the furniture which he had bought. I could look forward to some months of idleness before returning to India. There was a trout stream in the neighbourhood which would keep me occupied and out of mischief. We laid our heads together.

Jefferson did not want a house immediately, but bargains of that sort are not everyday affairs in these hard times. Besides, with me to share expenses for the next six months, the cost of living at Browdean Farm would be very low, and it seemed a profitable speculation to take the house then and there on a seven years' lease. This is just what Jefferson did—or rather, the agreement was signed by both parties within a week.

Rudge Jefferson and I were old enough friends to understand each other thoroughly, and make allowances for each other's temperaments. We were neither of us morose but often one or both of us would not be anxious to talk. There were indefinite hours when Rudge felt either impelled or compelled to write. We found no difficulty in coming to a working agreement. We did not feel obliged to converse at meals. We could bring books to the table if we so wished. Rudge could go to his work when he chose, and I could go off fishing or otherwise amuse myself. Only when we were both inclined for companionship need we pay any attention to each other's existence.

And, from the April evening when we arrived half an hour after the men with the furniture, it worked admirably.

We lived practically in one room, the larger of the two front sitting-rooms. There we took our meals, talked and smoked and read. The smaller sitting-room Rudge commandeered for a study. He retired thither when the spirit moved him to invoke the muses and tap at his typewriter.

Our only servant was the woman who had lately had charge of the keys. She came in every day to cook our meals and do the housework, and, as for convenience we dined in the middle of the day, we had the place to ourselves immediately after tea. The garden we decided to tend ourselves, but although we began digging and planting with the early enthusiasm of most amateurs we soon tired of the job and let wild nature take its course.

Our first month was ideal and idyllic. The weather was kind, and everything seemed to go in our favour. The trout gave me all the fun I could have hoped for, and Rudge was satisfied with the quality and quantity of his output. I had no difficulty adapting myself to his little ways, and soon discovered that his best hours for working were in the mornings and the late evenings, so I left him to himself at those times. We took our last meal, a light cold supper, at about half-past nine, and very often I stayed out until that hour.

You must not think that we lived like two recluses under the same roof. Sometimes Rudge was not in the mood for work and hinted at a desire for companionship. Then we went out for long walks, or he came to watch me fish. He was himself a ham-handed angler and seldom attempted to throw a fly. Often we went to drink light ale at the village inn, a mile distant. And always after supper we smoked and talked for an hour or so before turning in. It was then, while we were sitting quietly, that we discovered that the house, which was mute by day, owned strange voices which gave tongue after dark. They were the noises which, I suppose, one ought to expect to hear in an old house half full of timber when the world around it is hushed and sleeping. They might have been nerve-racking if one of us had been there alone, but as it was we took little notice at first. Mostly they proceeded from the kitchen, whence we heard the creaking of beams, sobbing noises, gasping noises, and queer indescribable scufflings.

While neither of us believed in ghosts we laughingly agreed that the house ought to be haunted, and by something a little more sensational than the sounds of timber contracting and the wind in the kitchen chimney. We knew ourselves to be the unwilling hosts of a colony of rats, which was in itself sufficient to account for most nocturnal noises. Rudge said that he wanted to meet the ghost of an eighteenth century miser, who couldn't rest until he had shown where the money was hidden. There was some practical use in that sort of bogie. And although, as time went on, these night noises became louder and more persistent, we put them down to 'natural causes' and made no effort to investigate them. It occurred to us both that some more rats had discovered a good home, and although we talked of trapping them our talk came to nothing.

We had been at the farm about a month before Rudge Jefferson began to show symptoms of 'nerves'. All writers are the same. Neurotic brutes! But I said nothing to him and waited for him to diagnose his own trouble and ease up a little with his work.

It was at about that time that I, walking homewards one morning just about lunch-time, with my rod over my shoulder, encountered the local policeman just outside the village inn. He wished me a good day which was at once hearty and respectful, and at the same time passed the back of his hand over a thirsty-looking moustache. The hint was obvious, and only a heart of stone could have refrained from inviting him inside. Besides, I believe in keeping in with the police.

He was one of those country constables who become fixtures in quiet, out-of-the-way districts, where they live and let live, and often go into pensioned retirement without bringing more than half-a-dozen cases before the petty sessions. This worthy was named Hicks, and I had already discovered that everybody liked him. He did not look for trouble. He had rabbits from the local poachers, beer from local cyclists who rode after dark without lights, and more beer from the landlord who chose to exercise his own discretion with regard to closing time.

P C. Hicks drank a pint of bitter with me and gave me his best respects. He asked me how we were getting on up at the farm. Admirably, I told him; and then he looked at me closely, as if to see if I were sincere, or, rather, to search my eyes for the passing of some afterthought.

Having found me guileless, as it seemed, he went on to tell me his length of service—he had been eighteen years on the beat—and of how little trouble he had been to anybody. There was something pathetic in the protestations of the middle-aged Bobby that, to all the world, he had been a man and a brother. He seemed tacitly to be asking for reciprocity, and his own vagueness drew me out of my depth.

You know those beautifully vague men, who pride themselves for being diplomatists on the principle that a nod is as good as a wink to a blind horse? The people who will hint and hint and hint, the asses who will wander round and round and round the haystack with hardly a nibble at it? He was one of them. He wanted to tell me something without actually telling me, to exact from me a promise about something he chose not to mention.

I found myself in dialectical tangles with him, and at last I laughingly gave up the task of trying to follow his labyrinthine thoughts. I ordered two more bitters and then he said, 'Well, sir, if anything 'appens up at the farm, you needn' get talkin' about it. We done our best. What's past is past, and can't be altered. There isn't no sense in settin' people against us.' I knew from his inflection on the word that 'us' was the police. He did not look at me while he spoke. He was staring at something straight across the counter, and I happened by sheer glance to follow the direction of his gaze.

Opposite us, and hanging from a shelf so as to face the customers, was a little tear-off calendar. The date recorded there was the nineteenth of May. Two evenings later—which is to say the evening of May the twenty-first—I returned home at half-past nine full of suppressed excitement. I had a story to tell Rudge, and I was yet not sure if I should be wise in telling it. His nerves had grown worse during the past two days, but after all there are nerves and nerves, and my talc might interest without harming him.

It was only just dusk and not a tithe of the stars were burning as I walked up the garden path, inhaling the rank scents of those hardy flowers which had sprung up untended in that miniature wilderness. The sitting-room window was dark, but the subdued light of an oil lamp burned behind the curtains of Rudge's study. I found the door unbarred, walked in, and entered the study. You see, it was supper-time, and Rudge might safely be intruded upon.

Rather to my surprise the room was empty, but I surmised that Rudge had gone up to wash. That he had lately been at work was evident from the fact that a sheet of paper, half used, lay in the roller of the typewriter. I sat down in the revolving chair to see what he had written—I was allowed that privilege—and was astonished to see that he had ended in the middle of a sentence. In some respects he was a methodical person, and this was unlike him. The last word he had written was 'the', and the last letter of that word was black and prominent as if he had slammed down the key with unnecessary force.

Two minutes later, while I was still reading, a probable explanation was revealed to me. I heard the gate click and footfalls on the path. Naturally I guessed that Rudge, temperamental as he was, had suddenly tired of his work and gone out for a walk. I heard the footsteps come to within a few yards of the house, when they left the path, fell softer on grass and weeds, and approached the window. The curtain obscured my view, but on the glass I heard the tap of finger-tips and the clink of nails.

I did not pause to reflect that Rudge, if he had gone out, must know that he had left the door on the latch, or that he could have no reason to suppose that I was already in the house. One does not consider these things in so brief a time. I just called out, 'Right-ho', and went round to the front door to let him in. Having opened the front door I leaned out and saw him—Rudge, I imagined—peering in at the study window. He was no more than a dark, bent shadow in the dusk, crowned by a soft felt hat, such as he generally wore. 'Right ho,' I said again, and, leaving the door wide for him, I hurried into the kitchen. There was some salad left in soak which had to be shaken and wiped before bringing it to the table. I remember that, as I walked through to the sink, one of the beams over my head creaked noisily.

I washed the salad and returned towards the dining-room. As I turned into the hall a gust of air from the still open door passed like a cool caress across my face. Then, before I had time to enter the dining-room, I heard the gate click at the end of the garden path, and footfalls on the gravel. I waited to see who it was. It was Rudge—and he was bareheaded.

He produced a book at supper, and sat scowling at it over his left arm while he ate. This was permitted by our rules, but I had something to tell him, and after a while I forced my voice upon his attention.

'Rudge,' I said, 'I've made a discovery this evening. I know how you got this place so cheap.'

He sat up with a start, stared at me, and winced.

'How?' he demanded.

'This is Stanley Stryde's old house. Don't you remember Stanley Stryde?'

He was pale already, but I saw him turn paler still.

'I remember the name vaguely,' he said. 'Wasn't he a murderer?'

'He was,' I answered. 'I didn't remember the case very well. But my memory's been refreshed today. Everybody here thought we knew, and the curious delicacy of the bucolic mind forbade mentioning it to us. It was rather a grisly business, and the odd thing is that local opinion is in favour of Stryde's innocence, although he was hanged.'

Rudge's eyes had grown larger.

'I remember the name,' he said, 'but I forget the case. Tell me.'

'Well, Stanley Stryde was an artist who took this place. He was what we should call in common parlance a dirty dog. He'd got himself entangled with the daughter of a neighbouring farmer—the family has left here since—and then he found himself morally and socially compelled to marry her. At the same time he fell in love with another girl, so he lured the old one here and did her in. Don't you remember now?'

Rudge wrinkled his nose.

'Yes, vaguely,' he said. 'Didn't he bury the body and afterwards try to make out that she'd committed suicide? So this is the house, is it? Funny nobody told us before.'

'They thought we knew,' I repeated, 'and nobody liked to mention it. As if it were some disgrace to us, you know! Oh, and, of course, the house is haunted.'

Rudge stared at me and frowned.

'I don't know about "haunted",' he said, 'but it's been a damned uncomfortable house to sit in for the past few evenings. I mean at twilight, when I've been waiting for you. My nerves have been pretty raw lately. Tonight I couldn't stand it, so I went out for a stroll.'

'Left in the middle of a sentence,' I remarked.

'Oh, so you noticed that, did you?'

'By the way,' I asked, 'what made you go out a second time?'

'I didn't.'

'But my dear chap, you did! Because the first time you came in you wore your hat, and two minutes later I saw you walking up the garden path without one.'

'That's when I did come back. I haven't worn a hat at all this evening.'

'Then who' I began.

'And that reminds me,' he continued quickly, 'when vow come in of an evening you needn't sneak up to the window and tap on it with your fingers. It doesn't frighten me, but it's disconcerting. You can always walk into the room to let me know you've come back.'

I sat and looked at him and laughed.

'But, my dear chap, I haven't done such a thing yet.'

'You old liar!' he exclaimed with an uneasy laugh, 'you've been doing it every evening for the past week—until tonight, when I didn't give you the chance.'

'I swear I haven't, Rudge. But if you thought that, it explains why you did the same thing to me tonight.'

I saw from his face that I had made some queer mistake, and interrupted his denial to ask, 'Then who was the man I saw peering in at the window? I saw him from the door. I thought you'd tapped at the window to be let in, not knowing that the door was open. So I went round and saw—I thought it was you—and called out, "Right ho."'

We looked at each other again and laughed uneasily.

'It seems we've got our ghost after all,' Rudge said half jestingly.

'Or somebody's trying to pull our leg,' I amended.

'I don't know that I should fancy meeting the ghost of a murderer. But, joking apart, the house has been getting on my nerves of late. And those noises we've always heard have been getting louder and more mysterious lately. '

As if to corroborate a statement which needed no evidence so far as I was concerned we heard a scuffling sound from the kitchen followed by the loud creaking of timber. We laughed again puzzled uneasy laughter, for the thing was still half a joke.

'There you are!' said Rudge, and got upon his legs. 'I'm going to investigate this.'

He crossed the room and suddenly halted. I knew why. Then he turned about with an odd, shamed chuckle.

'No,' he said, 'there's no sense in it. I shall find nothing there. Why should I pander to my nerves?'

I had nothing to say. But I knew that in turning back he was pandering to cowardice, because just then I would have done almost anything rather than enter that kitchen. Had anybody asked me then where the murder was done I could have told them with as much certainty as if I had just been reading about it in the papers.

Rudge sat down again.

'Don't laugh at me,' he said. 'I know this is all rot, but I've got a hideous feeling that things hidden and unseen around us are moving steadily to a crisis.'

'Cheerful brute,' I said smiling.

'I know. It's only my nerves, of course. I don't want to infect you with them. But the noises we hear, and the fellow who comes and taps at the window—they want some explaining away, don't they?'

'Especially now that we know that somebody was murdered here,' I agreed. 'I'm beginning to wish we didn't know about that.'

Rudge went early to bed that night, but I sat up reading. As often happens to me I fell asleep over my book, and when I woke I was almost in darkness, for the lamp needed filling. The last jagged, blue flame swelled and dwindled, fluttering like a moth and tapping against the glass. And as I watched it I became suddenly aware of the cause of my waking. I had heard the latch snap on the garden gate. And in that moment I began to hear them—the footfalls.

I heard the rhythmic crunch of gravel and then the swish of long grass and plantains, and then a shadow nodded on the blind. It loomed up large and suddenly became stationary. A loose pane rattled under the impact of fingers.

Perhaps there was a moon, perhaps not, but there was at least bright starlight in the world outside. The drawn blind looked like dim bluish glass, and the shadow of something outside was cut as cleanly as a silhouette clipped away with scissors. I saw only the head and shoulders of a man, who wore a dented felt hat. His head lolled over on to his left shoulder, just I had always imagined a man's head would loll if—well, if he had been hanged. And I knew in my blood that he was a Horror and that he wanted me for something.

I felt my hair bristle and suddenly I was streaming with sweat. I don't remember turning and running, but I have a vague recollection of cannoning off the door post and stumbling in the hall. And when I reached my bed I don't know if I fainted or fell asleep.

No, I didn't tell Rudge next day. His nerves were in a bad enough state already. Besides, in the fresh glory of a May morning it was easy to persuade myself that the episode had been an evil dream. But I did question Mrs Jaines, our charwoman, when she arrived, and I saw a look half stubborn, and half guilty cross her face.

Yes, of course, she remembered the murder happening, but she didn't remember much about it. Mr Stryde was quite a nice gentleman, although rather a one for the ladies, and she had worked for him sometimes. Stryde's defence was that the poor girl had committed suicide and that he'd lost his head and buried the body when he found it. Lots of people thought that was true, but they'd hanged Mr Stryde for it all the same. And that was all I could get out of Mrs Jaines.

I smiled grimly to myself. As if the woman didn't remember every detail!

As if the neighbourhood had talked of anything else for the two following years! And then I remembered the policeman's strange words and how he had been staring at the calendar while he spoke.

So that morning when I called at the inn for my usual glass of beer, I, too, looked at the calendar and asked the landlord if he could tell me the date of the murder.

'Yes, sir,' he said, 'it was May the' And then he stopped himself. 'Why, it was eight years ago, tonight!' he said.

I went out again that evening and came in at the usual hour. But that evening Rudge came down the path to meet me. He was white and sick-looking.

'He's been here again,' he said, 'half an hour ago.'

'You saw him this time?' I asked jerkily.

'Yes, I did as you did and went round to the door.' He paused and added quite soberly, 'He is a ghost, you know.'

'What happened?' I asked, looking uneasily around me.

'Oh! I went round to the door when I heard him tapping at the window, and there he was, as you saw him yesterday evening, trying to look through into the room. He must have heard me for he turned and stared. His head was drooping all on one side, like a poppy on a broken stem. He came towards me, and I couldn't stand that, so I turned and ran into the house and locked the door. '

He spoke in a tone half weary, half matter of fact, and suddenly I knew that it was all true. I don't mean that I knew that just his story was true. I knew that the house was haunted and that the thing which we had both seen was part of the man who had once been Sydney Stryde.

When once one has accepted the hitherto incredible it is strange how soon one can adapt oneself to the altered point of view.

'This is the anniversary of the—the murder,' I said quietly. 'I should think something—something worse will happen tonight. Shall we see it through or shall we beat it?'

And almost in a whisper Rudge said, 'Poor devil! Oughtn't one to pity? He wants to tell us something, you know.'

'Yes,' I agreed, 'or show us something.'

Together we walked into the house. We were braver in each other's company, and we did not again discuss the problem of going or staying. We stayed. I can pass over the details of how we spent that evening. They are of no importance to the story. We were left in peace until just after eleven o'clock, when once more we heard the garden gate being opened, and footfalls which by this time we were able to recognize came up the path and through the long grass to the window. We could see nothing, for our lamp was alight, but I knew what it looked like—the thing that stood outside had now tapped softly upon the glass. And in spite of having Rudge for company I lost my head and screamed at it.

'Get back to hell! Get back to hell, I tell you!' I heard myself shout.

And it was Rudge, Rudge the sensitive neurotic, who kept his head, for human psychology is past human understanding.

'No,' he called out in a thin quaver, 'come in. Come in, if we can help you.'

And then, as if regretting his courage on the instant, he caught my hand and held it, drawing me towards him.

The front door was locked, but it was no barrier to that which responded to the invitation. We heard slow footfalls shuffling through the hall, the footfalls, it seemed to me, of a man whose head was a burden to him. I died a thousand deaths as they approached the door of our room, but they passed and died away up the passage. And then I heard a whisper from Rudge.

'He's gone through into the kitchen. I think he wants us to follow.'

I shouldn't have gone if Rudge hadn't half dragged me by the hand. And as I went the sweat from the roots of my stiffened hair ran down my cheeks. The kitchen door was closed, and we halted outside it, both of us breathing as if we had been running hard. Then Rudge held his breath for a moment, lifted the latch, and took a quick step across the threshold. And in that same instant he froze my chilled blood with a scream such as I had heard in war-time from a wounded horse.

He had almost fainted when he fell into my arms, but he had the presence of mind to pull the door after him, so that I saw nothing. I half dragged, half carried him into the dining-room and gave him brandy. And suddenly I became aware that a great peace had settled upon the house I can only liken it to the freshness and the sweetness of the earth after a storm has passed. Rudge felt it, too, for presently he began to talk.

'What was he—doing?' I asked in a whisper.

'He? He wasn't there—not in the kitchen.'

'Not in the kitchen? Then what—who'

'It was She. Only She. She was kicking and struggling. From the middle beam, you know. And there was an overturned chair at her feet.'

He shuddered convulsively.

'She was far worse than he,' he said presently—'far worse.'

And then later, 'Poor devil! So he didn't do it, you see!'

Next morning we had it out with Mrs Jaines and we did not permit her memory to be hazy or defective. She must have known that we had seen something and presently she burst into tears.

'He said he'd found her hanging in the kitchen, poor gentleman, and that he'd buried her because he was afraid people would say he'd done it. But the jury wouldn't believe him, and the doctors all said that it wasn't time, and that the marks on her neck were where he'd strangled her with a rope. I don't believe to this day he did it, I don't! But nothing can't ever bring him back.' She paused at that and added. 'Not back to life, I mean—real life, like you and me, I mean.'

And that was all we heard and all we wished to hear.

Afterwards Rudge said to me, 'For his sake, the truth as we know it ought to be told to everybody. I suppose the police know?'

'Yes,' I said, 'the police know—now. But as Mrs Jaines said, it can't bring him back.'

'Who wants to bring him back?' exclaimed Rudge with a shudder. 'But perhaps if people knew—as we know—it might let him rest. I am sure that was what he wanted—just that people should know.'

He paused and drew a long breath through his lips.

'You write it,' he said jerkily. 'I can't!'

And so I have.

Furze Hollow

I

Hurlow came to stay at the Walmsley Arms on the eastern border of Jailbury Common for three reasons: he needed a country holiday; by going to Jailbury he was breaking fresh ground; and the inn was within walking distance of Moffat's cottage.

Moffat was a ripe scholar and a recluse, with antiquarian tastes. Hurlow had first met him on one of his infrequent visits to London, and had been immediately attracted to the older man. Moffat was a good talker when he chose, and Hurlow, who worshipped intellect, and whose lot in life was cast among dull and uninteresting people, hung upon his words.

The liking was mutual; possibly Moffat was not adamant against flattery which was obviously sincere. At least, he said suddenly to Hurlow, if you're ever down my way, I should be glad if you would come and see me.' This, as Hurlow learnt afterwards, was a rare remark for him to make.

Hurlow himself was a man of forty, who worked in a city office, and was one of those reserved, ungregarious beings who find it difficult to make friends. He was a bookworm who read unintelligently; his mind was always full of undigested letterpress. Almost his only recreation besides reading was to play chess. He generally spent his annual holiday walking, with a haversack half full of books. This July, however, for the reasons already stated, he settled himself on Jailbury Common.

Moffat disappointed him. He had expected Moffat to walk miles with him every day, and show him all the places of antiquarian interest. The older man, however, could not be persuaded to stir out of doors, and although it would not be fair to call him morose, Hurlow found it difficult to get him into a talking mood. He spent most of his evenings at Moffat's cottage, and passed most of his days—they were, fortunately, fine-weather days—walking, until he knew every path and nearly every tree and furze bush on the great tract of common land. He got to know, too, several of the local peasants, whom he described as 'characters'.

There was Walters, head-keeper on the manor estate, who enjoyed telling him amusing stories about the local worthies. And there was old Granny Light, who was supposed to be well over a hundred and to possess supernatural gifts. She had not walked for years, but during the spell of hot, fine weather she was to be seen in an armchair at her granddaughter's garden gate, white as a bone, shrunken and wrinkled, and seemingly incapable of coherent speech. Her lips moved continually in a meaningless mumble, and it was seldom that even her own kith and kin heard her speak distinctly.

It happened on a certain moonless night that Hurlow left Moffat's cottage at about half-past eleven, and turned his face towards the Walmsley Arms. That night he was more tired than usual, having exceeded the average extent of his walking exercise during the day.

The inn was nearly two miles distant by road, but there was a short cut to be made by following a footpath through copses, and over part of the common through a dip called Furze Hollow. He knew the path by daylight but, his sight being poor, he had not hitherto cared to trust finding his way in the dark by this shorter route. Tonight weariness held out an extra inducement, and he took the footpath.

Hurlow found his way through the two copses without much difficulty, and eventually climbed the stile which brought him out on to the open common in the light of the night sky. The night was bright, although moonless, for the stars shone clearly out of a cloudless sky, and it was easy to follow the line of the path as it wound among furze bushes. That part of the common was always lonely, although in the early evenings one might expect to pass one or two courting couples along the path.

Hurlow had walked only some twenty paces from the edge of the copse when his progress was arrested by a sound from the bottom of the hollow in front, low, thin, piercing, and almost startlingly sweet.

He came abruptly to a halt. He knew instinctively that these shrill, reedy notes were the music of pipes, and the environment lent magic to the sound. There in the dark, under the steadfast stars, the music shrilled and softened, and shrilled again. In such places and to such notes had Arcadian shepherds and shepherdesses danced. It was as if a poem had taken life and become tangible almost within his grasp.

But this was no lilting dance music. There was no air, only a succession of notes rising and dying away like so many separate lives, each independent of the others. Only in these thin, searching notes, there was the suggestion of one calling to another, as owl calls to owl across the dark.

All in a moment Hurlow forgot the beauty of the sounds and smelt fear. He smelt it as an animal smells it, the breath cold in his nostrils. He had read about Pan, a dead god who might safely be patronized while poring over a book in a London lodging, but here and at this hour a god not to be scorned. The half-conscious thought was a flash which died on the instant. Pan was dead. Voices had cried his death across the Aegean Sea. This was the twentieth century. And here was he, Hurlow, afraid because somebody chose to pipe at midnight upon a common. His fear, he had to admit to himself, was incontestable; but then he was a nervous and highly-strung man. In the ordinary way he would not have investigated the cause of the music, but the piper was somewhere in the hollow through which he had to pass, and to have turned back would have been a concession to the weaker side of himself. Nine men in ten would not have been nervous; Hurlow was, but he strode on all the same. There was good stuff in this highly-strung, imaginative bookworm.

He had not taken half a dozen steps before the piping ceased quite suddenly, with no warning of finality in the last note. Nor, as he went on, did he know if he were glad or sorry that it was not resumed. Music or no music, he might yet meet the piper.

When, a minute or two later, he reached the lip of the hollow, he saw before him in the middle distance, a flickering red light. He pressed on down the path, and presently made out in the dimness the outline of a caravan. He breathed suddenly for relief. It was only a gipsy encampment, after all, and a gipsy piper playing to the stars. He was not afraid of gipsies. They had a place of their own in romantic literature. He had read the works of George Borrow. He went forward more boldly.

At the bottom of the hollow, the drought-dried furze bushes grew sparsely, and there was ample room for a camp. Starlight and the glow of the camp-fire lit up the scene for him. Two caravans and two tents were there to leeward of the drifting wreaths of smoke; but none of the campers were astir or in sight.

Hurlow had been prepared for an exchange of civil goodnights, his nervousness gone. Now, seeing nobody, it unaccountably came upon him again. A furze bush scratched his legs as he hurried forward, lengthening his stride. If he could see nobody, he felt that others could see him—that he was watched by eyes which were neither inquisitive nor kind. A feeling of repulsion beset him and spurred him up the further slope of the hollow away from the camp. Not once did he look back.

Later, when he had reached the edge of the sandy road, and was within a furlong of the inn, he halted to light a pipe. Then he found that his hands trembled so that seven or eight matches flickered out in quick succession.

II

After breakfast, on the following morning, Hurlow, lighting his first pipe of the day, stepped out of the inn door on to the sunlit road.

The sun was already strong, for he had slept later than usual. Down the road, at the door of one of the cottages which clustered around the inn at this spot, where a peninsula of cultivated land ran into the wild, Granny Light was being carried to her chair by her granddaughter and great-granddaughter. From the other direction came Walters, the head-keeper, preceded by a mongrel, which made straight for Hurlow. The dog knew Hurlow for a friend and an occasional source of biscuits. Walters knew Hurlow for a London visitor who was generally willing to lay down the price of a pint of beer. He, therefore, gave him that salute which he normally reserved for the gentry. The head keeper stopped to chat, first growling at his dog, which was pawing at Hurlow's coat.

'You're havin' all the fine weather, sir. If you can't say you brought it 'ere, you can say you've kept it 'ere. Gerdaim, Rob, will yer! Just off out for a walk, sir?'

'Yes, I expect so. Didn't know you had gipsies on the common.'

'Oh, there's always them about. It's a job to get rid of 'em so long as you don't catch 'em doing nothin'. Why, have you seen some about, sir?'

'Yes, there's a camp down in Furze Hollow.'

The keeper's black little bushy eyebrows went up. Then he laughed.

'I reckon you got some of the names a bit mixed up, sir. Furze Hollow is the one place on this common where the gippos won't go.'

Hurlow pointed.

'Don't you call that Furze Hollow over there, with a footpath running through it to White's Copse?'

'Yes, that's Furze Hollow right enough, sir. But you ain't seen no gippos there.'

'Yes, I did. At least, I walked right through their camp.'

The keeper's little black beady eyes twinkled and grew smaller.

Wrinkles of laughter appeared at their comers.

'And what time was this, sir?' he asked.

'Close on midnight, I should think.'

'Ah, now! Come now, sir! You've been talking to Mr Moffat, you 'ave!'

Hurlow was mystified.

'I was at his house last night,' he said. 'It was on my way home that I passed the camp. '

Walters laughed. It was the smug, triumphant laughter of a man who catches another in the act of hoaxing him.

'Yes, and a nice camp and all you passed, sir!'

'What do you mean?'

'You try them jokes on somebody else, sir,' said Walters, still laughing.

'I crossed Furze Hollow at eleven o'clock, and there weren't no camp there then. No, sir, you'll have to try me with summat else. Kim 'ere, Rob, drat yer! Good mornin', sir—good mornin'. See you this evenin', perhaps, sir?

And don't you let Mr Moffat put you up to no more jokes, sir.'

He swung on, still laughing, leaving Hurlow mystified. He stood staring after the retreating figure with a puzzled smile. Then he walked leisurely in its wake towards the cottages.

A queer business, this, if what Walters said were true. Had the man really crossed Furze Hollow at eleven o'clock on the preceding night? Strange that the camp should have been pitched and fallen to silence, and the fire grown so mellow in that short time! And what did the fellow mean about his having been talking to Moffat, and perpetrating a joke? He had never felt less like joking in his life, and he had certainly seen the encampment. Besides, there was the piper.

Desultory steps brought him opposite to Granny Light, who sat propped up at her door, mumbling and mouthing as usual, with a patchwork quilt wrapped around her. Only this morning there seemed more light and life in her sunken eyes. He addressed her as usual in that tone which one generally uses to beings who can neither answer nor understand.

'Good morning, Mrs Light. How are you this morning?'

Her fifty-years-old granddaughter answered for her from the doorway.

'Granny's a bit better, thank you kindly, sir. She've been talkin' plainer, and she actually wanted to get up last night. I b'lieve she was strong enough to 'ave walked if we'd ha' let her. Wonderful 'twas. Maybe though, 'tis only the last flicker of the candle.'

Hurlow listened, his gaze on the old woman's face. Her eyes met his, and it seemed to him that she was addressing him. He bent his head to listen, and, for the first time, heard coherent words from her lips.

'I heered 'ee, boy. I heered 'ee. 'Tis the time come at last, and I be ready. '

'What is she sayin', sir?' the granddaughter demanded.

Hurlow did not repeat what he had heard. A shaft of cold had struck him through the sun's heat. He wished them good morning, and set out to walk sharply to Moffat's cottage. For reasons which he did not care to analyse he did not cross Furze Hollow, but took the longer way by road.

Moffat was neither washed nor fully dressed when he arrived. The recluse performed his toilet by instalments, so that it was rarely complete before the late afternoon. He welcomed Hurlow without enthusiasm, but the story which Hurlow unfolded awoke both his interest and his activity. He began feverishly to complete his toilet.

'Apparently,' Hurlow concluded, 'there's some story I don't know. Walters was sure that I had had it from you, and was using it to poke fun at him.'

Moffat paused in the act of fastening his collar. His eyes, under bushy grey brows, were alight with excitement, but a suspicious gleam stole into them.

'My friend,' he said, 'are you sure that you did not get the story from Walters, and are using it to poke fun at me?'

'Of course not. I know no story. Besides, am I that sort of man? For heaven's sake tell me what all this mystery is about.'

'I will tell you in good time, friend Hurlow. But first let us visit Furze Hollow. If there were an encampment there last night it will either still be there, or there will be traces of it. Come!'

They set off together through the copses, Hurlow trying all the way to induce Moffat to talk, and Moffat steadfastly refraining.

On the lip of the hollow Hurlow halted and exclaimed, 'They've gone!'

Gone indeed were the caravans and tents which he had seen on the preceding night. The cup-like hollow beneath him was deserted, save for a single figure in white flannels

'Yes, they've gone,' agreed Moffat, gnawing at his beard. 'And there's Lutford. Walters has lost no time in telling him.'

'Who's Lutford?'

'He's lord of the manor.'

'Do you know him, then?'

'I don't know anybody. I believe we nod to each other. Ah, he's seen us.'

Lutford had indeed seen them, and was making for them up the slope as fast as a pair of long legs could carry him at a walking pace. The decreasing distance revealed him as a young man with an aquiline nose, a narrow forehead, and features alike haughty and rather stupid. He nodded to Moffat when he had reached the pair, and addressed himself to Hurlow.

'Mr Hurlow, I believe?'

'That's my name.'

'Then will you have the goodness to tell me what you meant by telling my head-keeper that you saw gipsies here last night?'

'I told him that I saw a camp, and so I did.'

'Well, then, where is it? There has been no camp here. See for yourself. And in future I should be obliged if you would refrain from fabricating stones likely to disturb my tenantry. '

He brushed past them without another word, going the way they had come, leaving Hurlow too angry and amazed to speak.

Moffat laughed softly in his beard.

'There goes a superstitious man,' he said.

'Superstitious?'

'Not to believe, and still to fear, to half-believe, and scorn wholly to believe, that is to be superstitious. And now let us see if we can find any vestiges of your camp. From what Lutford said I do not think we shall.'

III

They searched the bottom of the hollow. There was no wheel-marks, no trodden grass, no traces of horses, no mark of tent-poles, nothing. A chill wind seemed to breathe on Hurlow. His face turned pale beneath its varnishing of sunburn.

'The camp-fire,' said Moffat; 'you say it was burning on the ground?'

'Yes.'

But they searched in vain for a burnt black patch in the open spaces among the parched, crackling furze. It might have been virgin ground, untouched since the beginning of time.

'By God!' cried Hurlow suddenly and hoarsely, 'there's something queer about this. I don't like it. What does it mean?'

'Sit down!' said Moffat, and lowered himself into a bed of dry bracken.

'Sit down and don't be afraid, and I'll tell you all that I know. It is foolish—superstitious if you like—to be afraid, for nothing can happen against Nature. Hitherto I have kept an open mind about this matter, neither believing nor disbelieving, but admitting frankly to myself that I did not know. Now I am beginning to believe. Calm yourself, Hurlow, and remember that this old world of ours is continually making fresh discoveries and forgetting old ones. We shall never know what the denizens of the lost continent of Atlantis knew. We may never re-discover the lost arts of the Magi, among whom it is almost certain astrology—to name but one—was an exact science. Our sciences would have astonished them; theirs would equally astonish us Only stray broken remains of the secret arts of the ancients survive. The witchcraft practised in the Middle Ages, and even in places still today, was all a blindfold stumbling after a cult at some time perfectly understood.'

He paused, and Hurlow, sinking down beside him, said breathlessly, 'I don't understand you. What are you driving at? Where are you leading me?'

'I am going to tell you an old story,' said Moffat. 'It is a well-authenticated story, of which your experience may well be the sequel. A hundred years ago, or close upon it, there was a gipsy encampment in this hollow. The depredations of these people aroused the ire of the local peasantry, who accused them of witchcraft, besides stealing. The squire—a Lutford in those days—at last ordered them to move, and in revenge they are said to have compassed by witchcraft the burning of the Manor House. Certain it is that the house was gutted in about two hours one night, and the house you see standing today is not above ninety years old.

'This burning of the Manor House brought matters to a head. The villagers, led by the squire, attacked the gipsies and burned out their camp here in this hollow. There is supposed to have been bloodshed. At least, one dying gipsy is said to have announced that they would return, and this return was naturally to be regarded as the portent of some dire happening to the Lutfords. The present-day gipsies know the story, for Furze Hollow bears an evil reputation with them, and none of them would think of camping here.

'Now, the gipsies left one girl-child behind them, who was picked up and adopted by a cottage woman who had just lost her own. And that child is Granny Light, who is still living today.'

Hurlow drew a sudden long breath.

'Good Lord!' he exclaimed. 'What are you telling me?'

'Now, this is very interesting and curious. Old Granny Light, in her day, was supposed to possess strange and unholy knowledge. She is said to have practised witchcraft, and the people about here, if you can get them to talk, will tell you of any number of miracles which she is supposed to have accomplished. Also she uttered a prophecy years ago to the effect that she would never die until her people came back for her; and you will remember that the dying gipsy had threatened their return. And here she is, still alive, perhaps a little more than a hundred years old, perhaps a little less.

'Well, there you have the story as accurately as I am able to recall it. Now, you know why Walters thought you were joking, and that I had already told you all this. And you know why Lutford, whom legend threatens with a calamity, was disturbed.'

Hurlow stared at him out of eyes which had grown watery with awe.

'Granny Light! And the piper seemed to be calling someone. She was restless last night, Moffat—wanted to get up. And this morning she said quite clearly, "I heered 'ee, boy. I heered 'ee. 'Tis the time come at last, and I be ready". '

Moffat's long, thin hands were pulling a frond of bracken to shreds.

'Did she say that?' he asked jerkily. 'And she wanted to get up, eh? Let's be calm about this, Hurlow, let's be calm and try to understand. To us may be given an experience unique among living men. Let us try to be worthy of it. Granny Light is a gipsy, and these gipsies are an old people who come from the East. They have little to do with the present, so it may be reasonable to assume that shreds of the old arts and practices remain with them. The gift of prophecy and some of the arts which we ignorantly call witchcraft may yet abide with them. You and I must be here tonight, Hurlow, there may be much to see. '

Hurlow bunched his handkerchief to wipe the sweat from his brow. When he spoke, his voice was like that of a man in pain.

'You have been talking. Words, words, words—I have hardly heard them. For God's sake tell me, Moffat, what you really think.'

'What I really think?' Moffat repeated. 'Well then,' he added calmly. 'I think that Granny Light's people have come back. I think the piper called her, and I think that somehow she will join them. And after that only God knows what is to happen. You will not be afraid to come here tonight?'

Hurlow left the question unanswered.

'I will come if you do,' he said.

Moffat rolled over in the bracken, gazing out over the common from which a flickering heat-vapour ascended.

'It seems so strange to you, so impossible,' he said. 'This is daylight, and the year is 1926. In a post-office two miles away they are using the telephone and telegraph. There is a race-meeting only ten miles distant. Some people would say that the things which we find ourselves believing could not happen in such times. We can only admit the incongruity.' He passed a hand over eyes half blinded by the sun, and said in another tone, and with seeming inconsequence, 'There will be another bad fire on this common unless we get some more rain soon, Hurlow.'

IV

Hurlow supped with Moffat that night, and they sat talking over the empty grate until nearly half-past eleven, when they set forth together on just such a night as the previous one. The moon had risen and set, but the cloak of night was spangled with stars.

All day Hurlow had been in a state of feverish excitement, but this had slowly subsided as the time for the actual adventure drew nearer. This was partly due to the fact that the strangest experiences in life are apt to lose their effect if dwelt upon long enough, and partly due to Moflat's demeanour, which remained soberly constant. Tilings might interest the little, bearded, satyr-like man, but they did not disquiet him. He lent confidence to Hurlow, who would have embarked with him on this adventure sooner than with any young giant who was armed to the teeth.

Neither spoke much as they breasted the heavy darkness of the copses, but Moffat's step was resolute, even sprightly. He was the eternal student going forth to learn. He was already astride the stile separating the second copse from the open common, when he suddenly ceased moving, and squatted upright on the top bar in a listening attitude. Hurlow, a pace or two behind him, saw him framed by an arch of the branches, a faun-like silhouette with uplifted finger.

'The pipes,' said Moffat just above his breath.

Hurlow heard the notes—shrill, thrilling, and soft by turn, and calling, calling, always calling. The magic of their sweetness scarcely touched him tonight, but he marked its effect upon Moffat, who lingered astride the stile for a long minute.

At last Moffat scrambled over, and Hurlow followed and trod on his heels, desperately anxious to keep pace over the narrow path between the furze bushes. And as they hastened, again the piping died away as suddenly as if the sound were cut off by the closing of a door.

On the edge of the hollow Moffat, who had kept the lead, suddenly stopped.

'There!' he said.

Hurlow looked over his shoulder, and below them, in the cup of the hollow, he saw the ruddy light of a camp-fire After a moment, since he already knew what to look for, he saw more than that. Starlight and the light of the fire conspired to show him dim shapes, which he recognised as tents and caravans. But down there, in that shadowland of furze and bracken, there was no movement nor any sign of life.

'What shall we do?' he whispered in Moffat's ear.

'You walked through it safely last night,' Moffat whispered without moving.

'Yes; but I couldn't tonight. Last night I didn't know'.'

Moffat turned and faced him. Outwardly he was calm; his only sign of fear was that he sweated like a frightened horse. Hurlow saw moisture like dew upon his forehead.

'Nor could I,' said Moffat simply. 'I could reason soundly on the folly of fear, but I would not walk through that hollow now for all the gold in the Indies.'

Something like panic struck at Hurlow. Moffat's calm confession of fear withdrew the prop upon which he had leaned. Down there, among the motionless shadows, lurked invisible things, things that were nameless, shapeless, and malignant; things which could see without being seen. One of the long-lost terrors of childhood returned to him, and like a child he put his hand into Moffat's.

'What are we to do?' he asked in a whisper, longing for Moffat to suggest that they should go.

'What can we do? It seems that we are only men and not heroes. We can only stay here and watch. '

A moment later Hurlow cried out as if a flame had scorched him. There was a sudden crackling of bracken, and a man's form appeared out of the darkness at his elbow.

'All right, sir! All right!'

It was Walters the head-keeper. His face was ghastly, and by no muscular effort could he control the chattering of his teeth.

'My dog—he ran away!' he whispered hoarsely. 'He knows! Mr Moffat, sir, for heaven's sake what does it mean?'

'I don't know.' Moffat's voice was shaken, but it sounded almost nonchalant to the other two. 'There seems to be a camp down there.'

'Yes; there was one last night, and none this morning. There was none here tonight, half an hour ago. I've been watching all day, and all this evening, and no gipsies on the move, and now—there's fire and caravans and tents. I crawled as near as I dare, but that dog of mine he howled and ran, and dogs know! I've had a scrap or two with poachers, and I've been through the war, but I'd sooner put my head in hell than go down that hollow.'

Neither Moffat nor Hurlow answered him. All three stood still, listening to the manifold little sounds which broke upon the silence of the night; the wings sighing in the feathery tops of bracken, the distant barking of a fox, the yet more distant crowing of an early cock.

'Gentlemen,' stammered Walters. 'You'll stand by me?'

'What can we do?' Hurlow growled.

'I got to warn the guv'nor that they're there. And I daren't move no more by myself. Don't stay 'ere, gentlemen. It ain't worth it. Nothin' ain't worth it.' Moffat glanced at Hurlow.

'Let's go with him,' he whispered; 'we can return.'

Walters knew his way about the common without paths. He knew all the little open strips between the furze bushes and the gaps between clump and clump. So he led them around the edge of the hollow and out on to the road.

His way lay past the inn, and, despite the lateness of the hour, the door of it was ajar, and the aperture faintly illumined by yellow candle-light. A woman, clasping a bottle, stepped back, calling out goodnight to somebody within. It was Mrs Hicket, the granddaughter of Granny Light. Hurlow stopped and asked, 'What's the matter?'

'It's granny, sir,' the woman explained. 'We've been having a trouble with her again. She've been sayin' as she must get up—her as haven't walked for ten years. I've been holdin' her, and terrible strong she've seemed. She's quiet again now, and sleepin', but I thought it best to get brandy in case she went faint-like after it all.'

She hurried on, calling out goodnights, and the three men exchanged meaning glances.

'We need not trouble to return to the hollow tonight,' said Moffat. 'Nothing will happen now.'

V

All next morning the glass fell, and in the afternoon there was a marshalling of clouds in the south and west—whither the wind had veered—which slowly spread themselves across the sky. The rumble of far-off thunder, like distant guns, was heard; but the storm circled about without breaking overhead, and no rain fell.

Moffat came over to sup at the inn, and afterwards spent much time at the window of Hurlow's private sitting-room, staring out into the night. Hurlow, smoking in an armchair, watched him, and presently inquired after the weather.

'I've seen lightning twice. If it would only rain!'

'Why?'

'I wish there would be a cloud-burst. I should like to see this parched land soaked and sluiced and flooded. I should like to see every ditch brimming and every pond over-flowing.'

'Because the land needs it?'

'Because young Lutford needs it. My friend, we can have no doubt that unless other powers intervene there is a tragedy impending for that young man. We have seen and heard enough to assure us that old Mrs Light's people have come back. They have made good half their threat by returning from the grave, or from hell, or from where you will. The other unuttered half, they have yet to make good. We are not, thank Heaven, encompassed by only evil powers, although it would seem that to evil is given a long tether. The last tragedy was by fire. Water is the enemy of fire, and if the rain falls in time this tragedy may yet be averted. But it will be a close race. We must be out earlier tonight.'

'Where?' Hurlow asked, puffing nervously at his pipe. 'I don't—I don't think I'll go to the hollow tonight.'

'Nonsense,' Moffat said gently. 'You have seen so much, and you must see the end. A storm is coming, and the storm will bring the rain. I think the end will be tonight.'

Moffat had his way, and the two set out just before eleven o'clock. And just at the junction of the footpath and the road they heard the distant sound of pipes.

'Ah!' whispered Moffat. 'As I told you. Early tonight.'

And tonight the pipes played clearly and sweetly and triumphantly on and on. Some notes broke and chuckled as with a lewd glee. And tonight the pipes called insistently, and yet played to a measure which tempted hands and feet to respond to the rhythm. Hurlow, scarcely knowing it, found himself marching springily to the beat of the tune; then came Moffat's hand on his arm, and Moffat's voice in his ear.

'For God's sake! Not this devil's dance!'

Louder, louder blew the pipes as they advanced towards the hollow. The sight of two figures ahead of them, standing on the edge of the dip, brought them to a sudden halt. Then Moffat, touching Hurlow's elbow, said, 'It is all right. They are Lutford and Walters. I know Lutford's way of leaning on his stick.'

The young squire and the keeper heard them approach, and came a little way to meet them. Lutford held out a trembling hand.

'Mr Hurlow,' he said, 'I beg your pardon for what I said to you yesterday. The unbelievable is true. It is good of you both to come tonight.'

Hurlow muttered something as the four pressed forward once more.

Minute by minute the piping grew louder, more alluring, more maddening.

'Has it been like this before?' Lutford asked, between his teeth.

'No,' muttered Hurlow. 'Only a few notes. Nothing like tonight.'

On the edge of the hollow they could see the camp-fire below, but the dark around it was impenetrable. For a long minute they stood silent, listening to the strange music and the laboured sounds of one anothers' breathing. Lutford at last heaved a long sigh.

'I can't stand any more of this,' he whispered. 'I'm going down.'

Instantly Moffat had him by the arm, and they made a curious picture for a moment—the little, frail, bearded man clinging to the tall, wiry youth.

'No, you're not!' he cried. 'Not while there are three of us to hold you. Walters—Hurlow—'

They all seized him, and, after a moment, Lutford tacitly surrendered.

'If I were you, Mr Lutford,' said Moffat sternly, 'I should be standing by my house tonight!'

'What—at home? With all this happening here?'

'You may be wanted there. Ah!' He uttered a suppressed cry. 'Did you see?'

A jagged vein of red lightning shot down from the sky, lighting the hollow for some immeasurable fraction of time.

'I saw caravans and tents,' Lutford muttered.

'Nothing else? Listen! The piper is on the move. He is marching to and fro. You can hear. Wait for more lightning, and watch.'

As if in response to a silent request from all of them came another flash, revealing to all four pairs of eyes the cup of the hollow.

So much and so little may be seen by a flash of lightning. The eye sees, but ere the brain can tell it what to look for the chance is gone. But what Hurlow saw will remain impressed upon his memory until the day of his death.

He saw human figures at the bottom of the hollow—perhaps a score of them—and all seemed to be swaying and gyrating to the measure of the pipes. While he still stared into the dark, Moffat clutched his arm.

'Look!' he whispered. 'That other light.'

There was another light now besides that of the camp-fire. It grew larger and larger as they stared. A tongue of flame shot up and vanished against the sky. Borne on the wind came the odour of sweet and pungent smoke.

'The furze!' cried Lutford suddenly. 'The furze is alight!'

The fire ran from bush to bush as if it followed a trail of oil. The light from a dozen blazes, which quickly merged into one crackling pool of fire, showed the smoke moving about it like a black cloak. But caravans and tents and people were gone. Only, in the midst of this sudden and growing waste of fire, the pipes played on sweetly, recklessly.

Great gusts of smoke blew into the faces of the four, but they stood watching, fascinated, unable to move, until at last Walters uttered a choking cry and pointed.

The fire had lit up all sides of the hollow, and thrown a wall of bright haze against the darkness around its edges. And as they stared, following the direction of the keeper's pointing finger with their gaze, they saw the bent figure of an old woman stumble into the radius of light not fifty yards away. Hurlow uttered a little gasp, and shut his eyes. He did not see what the others saw. They told him afterwards how the woman's figure, moving swiftly and resolutely, climbed down the slope and flung itself into the bath of fire, which straightway engulfed it. And on the instant the piping ceased and a blind terror came upon Walters, who uttered a sudden sobbing cry.

'Granny Light!' he cried, his voice rising to a scream. 'Granny Light!

Oh, God, it was Granny Light!'

He spun about on his heels and began to run stumblingly, and this panic communicated itself to the others, so that they blundered after him. It was not until they had gained the road that Lutford regained control over himself.

'We must wake the village,' he cried. 'We must save the common if we can. Come on!'

They began again to run, and were close by the inn when a frightened woman flung herself out of a cottage gateway across their path. It was Mrs Hicket.

'Granny's dead!' she wailed. 'Granny's dead! Oh, what shall I do?

Granny's dead! She wanted to get up again, and I was holding her when she died. And she shouting about the piper when the breath left her!'

A cry from the inn distracted them from the woman's half-hysterical clamouring. An upper window had been thrown open, and the landlord was leaning out and shouting at the top of his voice. He cried, 'Fire! Fire! Fire!'—the same word over and over again.

Lutford ran a few paces towards the window.

'Yes,' he shouted, 'we know. Come down, will you? The common!'

'No, not the common! Oh, look, sir!'

Away to the north they all saw another glare in the sky, and a sudden leap of flames showed them the face of a tall, long, white-fronted house. As the old Manor House had been burned out that night nearly a hundred years before so was the new one burned tonight. And by what agency? Who shall say?

The Man Who Made Haunted Houses His Hobby - The Severed Head

Derek Scarpe walked out into the lobby of the club, still fingering the card which a waiter had presented to him a few moments before. An elderly man of military appearance rose with a smile as Scarpe spoke his name.

'Colonel Rokeley?'

'Mr Derek Scarpe?'

Subconsciously the two men took each other's measure. The older had obviously been a soldier, upright, iron-grey, scrupulously dressed. Scarpe, used to summing up men at a glance, guessed him to be unimaginative, prosperous, and scrupulously upright and honest.

Scarpe's appearance, on the other hand, came as a surprise to the colonel. The idea of a man who made 'haunted' houses his hobby had conjured a picture of a tall, lean individual with pallid cheeks, sunken eyes, and long hair. Scarpe reminded him more of an athlete. He was a squarely built man of medium height, with a fresh colour, merry brown eyes, and short, crisp hair.

'Will you come into the lounge?' said Scarpe. "We can find a quiet comer, and talk over a cup of tea.'

He led the way through into a great room, about which were scattered half-a-dozen men dozing over newspapers or already asleep. At one end a fire smouldered in a huge grate, its embers pale in the full afternoon sunlight. Scarpe approached the fire, stirred it, pulled up two armchairs, and signalled to a passing waiter.

'Tea for two,' he said. 'Toast, Colonel Rokeley?'

'I thank you, no. If you don't mind I would sooner smoke than eat. Tobacco, I find, is more than ever a necessity when one is worried. . . . ' lie broke off. 'Mr Scarpe,' he added, 'it is more than good of you to receive me like this. I have come to you as a stranger. I only heard of you at second or third hand. I might have obtained a letter of introduction, but it would have taken time and'

'And time is often very valuable,' Scarpe said easily. 'Well, Colonel, please don't apologise I am very glad you wrote to me, and very glad to see you now. If I can help you I will promise to do all in my power. I should like to know, though, why you came to me.'

The other smiled wanly.

'Because,' he said, 'you don't accept money for your services. It isn't that I'm not prepared to pay, but these fellows who make Spiritualism a trade are being shown up every day. I told myself that you might be mistaken, but that you must be honest.'

Scarpe nodded. The waiter returned with tea, and he kept silent until the man had gone.

'Now, Colonel Rokeley,' he said, 'first of all I want to tell you that I am not a medium, nor do I profess to be any kind of a mystic. I know this, however, that people do sometimes return from death and manifest themselves in strange and terrible ways.'

'Strange and terrible!' the colonel murmured. 'Yes, I think I should have used those two adjectives if you had not.'

'Suppose now,' said Scarpe, 'you had gone away on a long journey, from which it was very difficult, even painful for you to return. Tell me what would bring you back? No, I will tell you. Bad trouble at home—sickness, death, or the knowledge that things were happening which saddened or angered you. Colonel Rokeley, that is why sometimes people come back from the longest journey of all—that journey across the Three Rivers. All that we can do is to try to discover what brings them back, and readjust things so that they can rest in peace. That is the way I set about "laying" ghosts, and I have often been successful. Now please tell me your story from beginning to end in your own way.'

The colonel was smoking a cigar. He leant back, stretched his long legs, and focussed the gaze of his half-closed eyes on the glowing end.

'Mr Scarpe,' he said. 'I never believed in ghosts. I always said I'd believe in them when I saw one, and even now that I've seen—something, I don't want to believe. But I suppose I must. This morning I went to see Blake and Reval, the great illusionists, and asked them if they could produce phenomena, such as I have described, and in such circumstances. They admitted that they could not If they could not, nobody could. There can be no trickery.

'Now to the story. I am an old Anglo-Indian. I retired from the Indian army six years ago on the death of a cousin who left me a great deal of property, including Dodfield Hall in Lincolnshire. I went to live there with my wife and my three daughters.

'Dodfield is a very old house with a place in history. In the Great Civil War the Dodfields espoused the Royal Cause, and so spirited a fight did they make, that Sir Charles and Lady Mary held out until late in 1646, a year after the battle of Naseby. The Governor of Lincoln then took strong action, and besieged the gallant couple with large forces of pikemen and musketeers, backed by artillery. I can show you today where the damage done by cannon shot has been repaired. The house fell after Sir Charles had been shot dead by a musket-ball at one of the windows.

'The conquerors were not disposed to be merciful to a gallant foe. Frightful deeds of savagery followed the fall of the garrison. Lady Mar, to save her husband's body the indignity of being quartered and hung in chains in Lincoln, had caused it to be hidden or buried. For her refusal to disclose its hiding-place the brutes beheaded her in the entrance hall. Perhaps it is no wonder that the place was always supposed to have a ghost.

'Yes, Dodfield Hall was always supposed to be haunted, although the Dodfields, so far as I know, are extinct. As a boy I used to stop there, but I never saw Lady Maiy, nor did I ever meet anyone who had actually seen her. It was the same when I inherited the place. People still said that it was haunted, but I never met anyone who had even heard of a single instance of the apparition having been seen. We spent more than five years there without being troubled in any way. Then, just over a month ago, the trouble started. The servants have nearly all gone, and I can't blame them. I've sent my wife and daughters down to Bournemouth. I'm sticking it out, but, my God, Mr Scarpe, sometimes the horror gets hold of me . . . like a cold hand! I can't stand it much longer.'

There was a short silence. Then the colonel went on:

'Everybody in the house has been terrified during the last few weeks, by the apparition of a woman's head. There is no particular place or time to expect it. Sometimes it is invisibly suspended in mid-air, sometimes one will suddenly see it resting on a chair or a table. I have walked into my bedroom and seen the loathsome thing on my pillow. It looks perfectly tangible, but when I have tried to seize it, it has melted through my fingers and vanished. As I said, it appears in no particular room and at no particular time after sundown, but you can scarcely spend a night in the house without seeing it.'

He paused, and Scarpe nodded gravely.

'Can you describe it to me?' he asked.

'Oh, yes! It is the head of a middle-aged woman. The hair is iron-grey and cut short. I suppose they would have cut it short before they made her bend over the block. The skin is yellowish white, the complexion of the dead, but the eyes and the mouth—there is nothing dead about them! I have never seen such awful malevolence as those eyes express. And, though never a word is uttered, the lips gibber spite and hatred at one. Poor woman, she didn't die at peace with the world, and loving her enemies.'

Scarpe lit a cigarette.

'How many times have you seen this apparition, Colonel Rokeley?' he asked.

'Perhaps twenty or thirty.'

'Who else has seen it?'

'My wife and daughters and all the indoor servants.'

'And you're living there alone?'

'Not quite. My new butler has turned out a splendid fellow. He was in the Guards—an officer's servant—and he doesn't know what nerves are. I've induced two of the maids to sleep at one of the lodges, and they come in every day and do the cooking and a little of the necessary housework.'

Scarpe regarded his guest with a certain measured admiration.

'Colonel Rokeley,' he said, 'you are a very brave man.'

'It's not that.' The old soldier heaved his great body, it's my house,' he cried, raising his voice a little. 'I won't be driven out by anyone, alive or dead. My house! Why should I go?'

'Why should you, indeed? Well, it was plucky of you to stay, because it was something you didn't understand.'

'Do you understand it?'

'I think so. I suppose you want me to come down. Will tomorrow do?'

'Excellently. It's more than kind of you.'

'Not at all. I am obsessed by this sort of thing. One more question, if you please, before we close the subject for the time being. This butler, who is staying on with you is new, you say. How long have you had him?'

'Not much more than a month. He arrived almost at the same time that the manifestations began.'

'Ah!'

The colonel looked up.

'I must beg of you,' he said, 'not to suspect him of being the cause of these manifestations. He came to me with an excellent character. He can have no end to serve by driving us all out of the house. Moreover, even the greatest conjurers in the world cannot produce such an illusion in just the same manner as I have described to you. '

'I didn't suspect him of producing any illusions,' Scarpe answered.

They set off from London on the following day, and were at Dodfield in time for a late luncheon.

Dodfield Hall was one of those repellent-looking old houses that one would expect to have a reputation for being 'haunted'. It was built partly of stone and partly of mellow red brick, the stone part dating back to the fourteenth century. Two hundred years later the house had been added to and partly rebuilt. Here and there the masonry was patched with brickwork of a slightly deeper hue, a testimony to the damage done by the queer little cannon of the period what time the house stood siege for the lost cause of King Charles.

The house had been built in the bend of a small river, which formed a natural moat around three sides. At some period a little canal had been dug, so that today the building was surrounded by a ring of water. The river wound away from this ring, like the tail of a capital Q, to feed a lake half a mile behind the house. In ancient warfare Dodfield must have been a difficult place to take, and seeing it, Scarpe realised how it had held out so long.

Glossop, the butler, let them into the self-same hall where poor Lady Mary Dodfield had so gallantly laid down her life nearly three hundred years before.

'Any news?' Colonel Rokeley asked.

'Well, sir, I've had to deal with some sightseers and one or two ladies and gentlemen who wanted to spend a night here. I sent them off quick, as you told me, sir.'

The colonel sighed.

'I suppose the papers will get hold of this soon,' he said. 'Glossop, this gentleman has come to try and remove the—er—the disturbance. If he tells you to do anything, do it.'

'Very good, sir.'

'Have you seen it again?'

'Oh, yes, sir, often! I reckon, sir, I see it more than anybody else, and it looks at me different from the way it looks at others—more hateful like. Last night it got me a bit groggy, and I had a job to persuade myself it wasn't going to hurt me in some way. But, Lord, sir, if it could have hurt me it 'ud have done that long ago!'

Scarpe regarded the man narrowly. He was tall, of a medium colouring, and rising forty. His eyes were clear, entirely fearless, and looked out frankly but not obtrusively. The most suspicious detective would have required strong evidence before he suspected Glossop of complicity in any crime.

'Luncheon can be served as soon as you wish, sir,' said the man, as calmly as if they had just been discussing a cricket match.

Colonel Rokeley and his guest talked little over the meal, which was laid at one end of a great oval table.

'I suppose,' the colonel remarked, 'there is nothing for us to do but wait until tonight.'

'I'm not so sure,' Scarpe answered. 'I suppose you have not, by any chance, any written record of the siege of the house, and the subsequent tragedy. I should like to get, if I could, a really detailed account.'

'I have nothing myself,' the colonel answered, 'but I can certainly help you. The vicar of this parish at the time kept a diary, in which is to be found a very detailed account of the siege. That diary is preserved in the museum attached to the public library over at Redthorpe, four miles away. I have some small influence there, and the curator will allow you to examine the manuscript if you show him my card, which, of course, I will give you. If you wish I will drive you over.'

'Thanks,' said Scarpe; 'but if you don't mind I would sooner go alone. The sooner the better, so I'll set off directly after lunch.'

'Very well. If you can drive a small Humber, there's one in the stables, and you can drive yourself over when you please. You'll be back by dusk.'

'Oh, certainly! Once I get hold of that diary it won't take me long to find out what I want to know, provided it contains the information. I've got a theory already, which I have hopes of developing.'

'My dear sir, you haven't even yet seen the apparition!'

'I can take that for granted. By the way, there is a small item of expense attached to what I have in view. I suppose you don't object. It'll only amount to a few pounds, ten or twenty at the most.'

The colonel waved his hand.

'Go ahead,' he said. 'I am not a poor man, and I'd give half my money to get this appalling business settled and done with.'

So it happened that in the afternoon Scarpe drove himself over to Redthorpe and visited the public library. He was back by five o'clock, and in high spirits.

'That diary,' he said, 'is a wonderful piece of work. It deserves a place on the same shelf as the writings of Pepys and Evelyn. Apart from that it's told me just what I wanted to know. And now I want to ask your butler a question or two.'

Glossop, summoned by the bell, duly appeared. Scarpe turned to him with a smile.

'Now,' he began, 'I'm going to ask you rather a curious question or two. You'll wonder why I'm asking them, and you may think I suspect you of trickery of some sort in the matter of the disturbances here. But I assure you that I'm as certain of your innocence in that respect as you are yourself. I want to know your full name—your Christian names.'

'Thomas Henry, sir,' said Glossop stolidly.

'What was your mother's maiden name?'

'Woodger, sir.'

'Where were you born, and in what year?'

'Parish of Stockcross, near Newbury, in Berkshire, sir, in the year 1879.'

'Thank you, Glossop, that's all I want to know for the present I'll explain to you in good time why I asked for these details of your family history. Sorry to have had to do it.'

'I hope, sir, you don't think'

'Glossop, if you ever lose your job here, come to me. And may you stick to me in my hour of trouble as you're now sticking to your present master! That's what I think of you.'

Glossop departed gratified by the compliment, but greatly puzzled, as was his master.

'I won't bother you,' said the colonel, 'by asking questions now. Come into the smoke-room. If you play ecarte, I'll try to give you a game. Or, unless you're a rather exceptional player, I think I could owe you twenty-five in a hundred up at billiards.'

'We'll try both,' Scarpe laughed. 'Ecarte first, if you will.'

They played for a couple of hours, and then Colonel Rokeley glanced at his watch.

'If you care to change the game now,' he said, 'there's just time for a hundred up before we put on our dinner jackets. I've a good table.'

Scarpe, who was apparently willing to be entertained by anything, followed his host up the staircase to a great room on the first storey, once an apartment for honoured guests, and now a billiard-room.

Colonel Rokeley entered first and switched up the lights. Then he uttered an exclamation and stepped back, treading on Scarpe's feet.

'Look there! Look there!' he said quickly and tensely.

The touching of the switch had caused six heavily shaded lights over the table to throw all their light upon the heavy cloth which protected the baize from dust and dirt. In the middle of the table in full glare of the lights stood balanced on its neck a woman's head, almost strangely solid-looking in that brilliant illumination.

The hair was short and grey, the skin death-colour, but the eyes were alight and alive and seemed to give out actual rays of hatred. The grey lips, while they emitted no sounds, twisted and gibbered, as if curses and cries of hatred were being wrung from them.

Scarpe stepped past the colonel and approached near the table. He stood gazing at the head a full half-minute.

'I don't wonder,' he remarked, 'that all the servants except Glossop left you.'

An unlit cigarette was in his mouth, and he struck a match. Then, moving backwards to the rack, he seized a cue, and taking a few steps forward again he made a jab at the head. It was as if the cue had been a magician's wand, for the head vanished like an extinguished flame.

Scarpe went early to bed that night, and was rummaging in his larger suit-case for a collar for the morrow's wear when a glance over his shoulder brought him to his feet and turned him half-about. In an armchair by the grate rested the head, exactly as he had seen it on the billiard-table. He stood motionless for half a minute, watching it as before. Then he spoke, but not to the apparition. It was as if he was addressing somebody in thought a long distance away.

'Lady Mary,' he said slowly and distinctly, 'I have very little hope that you can hear me. I know that head is not you. It is projected here by your anger and your woe. if you can hear me, learn this, that I know what troubles you, and I will remove the cause of it, so that henceforward, dear, brave and loyal lady, you shall rest in peace. '

Almost before he had ceased speaking the head was gone, and at breakfast next morning he thought the occurrence scarcely worth mentioning to his host.

'Today,' he said, 'we are going to try, with your permission, a little experiment. I want you to send Glossop off for two or three days.'

The colonel sighed.

'I can't think,' he said, 'why you suspect that man of playing a trick on us.'

'I don't.'

'Then why send him away?'

'Because I want to see if there are any apparitions in his absence.'

'I don't follow you, I must confess. You seem to contradict your own words. You think if I dismiss the man the house will be peaceful again.'

'I am nearly certain of it. But don't do anything yet. I am out to prove something.'

So Glossop was sent down to Bournemouth to collect some of his master's clothes which had somehow been packed with other luggage and been sent to Bournemouth with Mrs Rokeley and the three girls. At Scarpe's request he was told that he need not return for four days.

'You've had a tough time,' said the colonel, without meeting the man's gaze, 'and a day or two's absence from this beastly house will do you good. I shall be all right with Mr Scarpe.'

That night there were no manifestations of any kind, and Colonel Rokeley went to bed rather puzzled and greatly relieved.

Nor did the head appear at any time on the following two nights, and the colonel, although he would not admit more than the coincidence, was a little troubled in his mind concerning the faithful Glossop.

On the morning of the day when Glossop was due to return, Scarpe received a letter.

'I was right,' he said, laying it down. 'You will most definitely have to get rid of Glossop. And the firm of Willetson have sent in a bill for fifteen pounds, which, I suppose, is fairly reasonable.'

'Willetson's? Aren't they private detectives?'

'They are. And they've sent me some interesting news about Glossop.'

The colonel rose majestically.

'I warn you,' he said, 'I shall find it very difficult to believe anything against that man.'

'There is nothing against him. He has stuck to you like a true sportsman. It isn't a bit his fault that he's a descendant of the man who struck off Lady Mary's head.'

'Good God!'

'In that diary I found four interesting names. There was the name of the officer commanding the force that captured the house, the name of the soldier who shot Sir Charles, the name of the governor of Lincoln, and the name of the man who beheaded Lady Mary. The last man's name was George Teague. I sent the four names to Willetson's, and instructed them to trace Glossop's pedigree and see if he were descended from one of these four men. It transpires that one George Teague of Lincoln—born in 1622, died in 1701—is an ancestor of his on his mother's side. Well, it seems poor Lady Mary can't rest while one of the same blood as her murderer is in the house, so if you or she are to have any rest, Glossop will have to go.'

'But what on earth set you off on that track at the very beginning?'

'Well, you and your family had been here for some time without trouble of that kind until Glossop arrived. Obviously it had something to do with him. I'm sorry for Glossop. He's a good chap.'

'He is,' said the colonel, 'and I can thank him for the way he stood by me in a practical manner.'

In the course of time Glossop was set up in one of the jolliest little inns for motorists on the Portsmouth road

Mrs Rokeley and her daughters returned to Dodfield, and are probably still there, for it ceased abruptly from being a 'troubled' house.

The Man Who Who Made Haunted Houses His Hobby - The House of Treburyan

Treburyan rose quickly as Derek Scarpe was announced, and crossed half way to the door to meet him.

'This is very good of you, Mr Scarpe,' she said. 'I am so glad that you were able to come. Martin, another cup and saucer. I was just having tea.

We didn't know when to expect you, or of course we would have sent to meet you at the station. You must have had a very trying journey.'

Scarpe laughed. His fresh colour, merry brown eyes, and short, crisp hair seemed strangely out of keeping with his love of investigating the mysteries of haunted houses. 'To tell the truth, Miss Treburyan,' he said, 'I rather enjoyed it. We did Plymouth in less than five hours, and I still take a childish delight in travelling by fast trains. I had lunch on board, and that split the journey into two short halves.'

'Well, please come over and sit near the fire. You would like a cup of tea before going to your room, wouldn't you?'

'Thanks, I should. You've given me the room, I hope?'

'Oh, yes, Mr Scarpe. We took you at your word.'

The parlour-maid re-entered the room with a cup and saucer, and they were silent until she had departed.

'You mustn't think,' said Sylvia Treburyan, showing a faint colour in her cheeks, 'that we are a very queer household because I am here alone to receive you. My brother has been obliged to rejoin his regiment. I have bowed to the conventions so far as to have a companion. Mrs Saunders has gone out for a walk, but she'll be back presently. Would you sooner wait until you are not so tired before hearing'

'Really,' Scarpe interrupted smiling, 'I am not a bit tired. Besides, I am very anxious indeed to hear your story.'

'You must have read something of what I will call the introductory part in the papers?'

'Oh, yes. I will tell you exactly what I learnt from them. Mr Peter Treburyan, whom I take to be your uncle, mysteriously disappeared one afternoon about a month ago. He was an elderly and a studious man, something of a scholar, of a kindly and generous nature, and entirely without enemies. Nobody saw him leave the house. The ground attached to this house goes down to the cliffs, and it believed that he fell over and was washed out to sea when the tide came up. The mystery attached to his disappearance is increased by the statement made by his friend, Admiral Snode, who said that he was walking on the beach that afternoon, about half-a-mile distant from the gap called Hunter's Cove. He had with him a pair of powerful glasses. Looking through these he saw Mr Treburyan on a ledge of rock in the cove, about half way up the cliff. Amazed at seeing him in such a place he hurried forward, but the irregularities of the coast-line hid Mr Treburyan from view for a time, and when he reached the cove he had disappeared. He waited in vain. Had Mr Treburyan fallen, therefore, he must have been lying on the sand at the bottom of the cliff, but there was no visible trace of him. To add to the mystery the face of the cliff is so precipitous that there is no one in these parts who could reach that ledge, either from above or below, without ropes and climbing irons. I understand that it would have been regarded as almost an impossible feat for a young man to have performed; and Mr Treburyan was not only elderly, but suffered from heart trouble.'

Sylvia Treburyan inclined her head.

'You have learnt from the newspapers,' she said, 'just the literal truth. I know my uncle to be dead, and it is better for his death to be proved That afternoon I heard him call for help from a great distance. Since then I and others have seen his—his ghost. That is why I solicited your help. If we could only learn how he met his end, and find the body.

She came suddenly to a pause. Something of the strain under which she had laboured for the past few weeks showed itself in her face and in her speech.

Scarpe looked upon her with unobtrusive sympathy. She was tall and beautiful in a rather dark and stately fashion. She wore a high-waisted dress of black silk, with the opening at the throat cut low. Her lips and the pallor of her face suggested red and white roses. She had that wonderful blue-black hair which suggests the presence of Italian or Spanish blood.

'Now, please,' said Scarpe, 'tell me the rest. You know what I know. I want to hear your own story, the story that has not been put into print.'

The girl hesitated a moment.

'I don't quite know how to begin,' she said. 'If six weeks ago anybody had told me these things I should not have believed them. I can hardly hope that you'

Scarpe's smile was reassuring.

'Please don't trouble yourself on that score,' he said. 'Believe me, I have heard some very strange stories in my time, and proved them to be true, besides having myself seen some very strange things.'

'Well, my uncle withdrew from the dining-room after lunch on the seventh of last month, and was not seen alive by any of us again. His habit was to spend his afternoons undisturbed in the library. He went there for a while that afternoon, for we found the butt of his cigar in an ash tray. After that Heaven only knows what became of him. It was usual for him to come down to the drawing-room at about half-past four for a cup of tea. At about four o'clock Martin, the maid you have just seen, came in looking very scared, and complained about queer knockings she and the other maids had heard on the walls all over the house. She said she thought it was a sign that something dreadful was going to happen. I laughed at her, and said I would tell the master when he came down to tea, and that doubtless he would be able to explain it.

'When tea arrived at half-past four my uncle had not come down, so I ran up to call him. The quickest way from here to the library, as you will see when you go over the house, is up the servants' stairs. This, like all such staircases, is steep and very narrow. I had gone up about half way when I distinctly heard my uncle's voice crying out. He seemed to be speaking at my elbow, and yet, if you can understand me, the voice sounded miles and miles away. "Help !" he cried, "Help !" This was not imagination, Mr Scarpe. I did hear his voice, so close and yet so distant, cry those very words.

'My heart began to beat very violently, and I called out something in reply. But I heard no other sound, and, going up into the library, found it empty. Later, when our anxiety became intense, we searched the house and grounds, and the entire neighbourhood, but no sign of his earthly body has been seen from that hour to this.'

Scarpe inclined his head. 'But I understand from your letter,' he said, 'that you complain of certain disturbances.'

A strained look came into the girl's eyes.

'Mr Scarpe,' she said, 'you may believe it or not as you like, but we in this house have nearly all seen my uncle's ghost. If you stay here you cannot fail to see it too. It is driving us mad, or it will if this goes on. Mrs Saunders was the first to see it. She was going to bed on the following night when she met the wraith of my poor uncle in the corridor outside his room. His hands were pressed against his chest as if he were in pain, and he went before her to the door of the bedroom he had occupied in life, looking round at her from time to time as if he wished her to follow, but she was too frightened. On the night following I had exactly the same experience.'

'You are quite sure,' Scarpe inquired, 'that what you saw was not your uncle in the flesh?'

'Oh, quite! He was little more than a grey shadow, but it was impossible not to recognise him. I saw him another night, and the maids have seen him too. My brother came home on leave, and spent a night in that room, and his experience aged him terribly. He told us afterwards that he woke in the small hours to see our uncle standing beside his bed. His eyes seemed to beg my brother to get up and follow him, but fear kept him where he was.

The shadowy figure of my uncle then went over to the wall close to the fireplace, looked round appealingly at my brother, and vanished '

Scarpe took out his cigarette case, glanced at the girl, who nodded permission, and began to smoke. He was silent a long while. When at last he spoke it was to propound his theory in a low and gentle voice which Sylvia Treburyan found strangely pleasant and soothing.

'I believe,' he said, 'that when those who have crossed over return to this world it is generally because some mundane matter is troubling them. The first thing to do is to discover the cause of their trouble. In this case it is quite simple. You know your uncle to be dead, but he is still alive in the eyes of the law, and he will be legally alive for some time yet unless his body is discovered. Meanwhile, things are doubly hard for those he has left behind. Uncertainty is more trying than certain knowledge that the worst has happened; besides which no will can yet be proved, and there are a thousand and one harassing difficulties. Yes, I think your uncle will rest peacefully enough when we have discovered his body. '

'But where can it be? Do you think he has met with foul play?'

'That remains for us to discover. Tell me, are there any legends about the house? Had it a reputation for being haunted before these phenomena took place?'

'Yes. It is a very old house, you know, and the Treburyans built it for themselves in the reign of Elizabeth. They must have been, on the whole, a wicked family, and there are some dreadful stories of their doings. It is an open secret that the family fortune was founded on and maintained by smuggling. Of course smuggling was rife all along this coast until early in the nineteenth century, and even later. '

'Ah!' Scarpe sat up with a jerk, as if a sudden thought had struck him.

'I have heard it said,' continued the girl, 'that my great-grandfather was the first head of the family to live strictly within the law. Smuggling, so far as the Treburyans were concerned, ceased as soon as the property came into his hands. The room which my uncle used as a bedroom was supposed to be haunted, but none of us ever believed in it, and my uncle was never disturbed in any way.'

'And that is the room in which your brother claims to have seen your late uncles' wraith?' inquired Scarpe.

The girl inclined her head, and Scarpe nibbed his hands thoughtfully on his knees.

'What puzzles me so desperately is how he appeared to Admiral Snode half-way up the cliff in Hunter's Cove that afternoon '

'It all fits in admirably with the theory I have formed,' Scarpe assured her.

'You have a theory then?'

'Yes, and one which will disappoint me very much if it does not put us on the right track. Your uncle was alive and well when Admiral Snode saw him. It was no wraith which the admiral saw on the cliff.'

'But it must have been. You ought to see the place.'

'I don't even need to do that. Those knockings that the maids heard were not supernatural noises. That voice you heard crying out was your uncle's living voice.'

'But it could not have been! And the figure of my uncle that all of us have seen—are you going to tell me that that was his living self.'

Scarpe smiled sadly and shook his head. 'No, I am not,' he answered. 'I am quite sure that he is dead, and that what you have all seen since that afternoon is his disembodied spirit. Let me test my theory a little further. I wonder if I can tell you something that will surprise you.'

'Please go on.'

'After your uncle's disappearance a candle and candlestick were found to be missing from his bedroom.'

Sylvia Treburyan sat up with a start and seemed to stiffen in her chair.

'Mr Scarpe,' she cried out in amazement, 'who could have told you that?'

'Nobody told me.'

'I thought you expressly stated in one of your letters that you did not claim to be clairvoyant, and disbelieved those who professed to be. '

'So I did; so I do. You must pardon me, Miss Treburyan, for mystifying you a little. I don't like to speak of my theories before I have proved the truth of them, in case I should be wrong. If my theory were correct, then I should expect to hear that a candle was missing from your uncle's room. I find it is so, and that takes us a step further. Just one more word about the late Mr Treburyan. He suffered from heart trouble, I understand, and that, I may tell you now, I believe to have been the cause of his death. Can you give me any details as to his complaint.'

'Yes, it was valvular disease of the heart, and my poor uncle had to be very careful. Undue excitement, shock, or fatigue was liable to bring on an attack. Medical advice informed him that these attacks were always dangerous, but that, on the other hand he might live to a great age and die of some other complaint?'

Scarpe inclined his head as if she had spoken his own thought.

'I should like,' he said, 'if it wouldn't be troubling you too much, to see your late uncle's bedroom—this room that was supposed to be haunted before this present trouble arose.'

'I will take you there immediately,' she said.

Sylvia Treburyan sprang up.

Scarpe rose and made a movement towards the door, then he halted and turned.

'Do you know,' he asked, 'if there is such a thing as a long tape measure in the house? The kind of thing you use for measuring tennis courts before marking them off?'

'We ought to have one,' the girl answered. 'I'll go and see.'

She hurried out, and returned after a few minutes with the required article, and asked if he were ready to accompany her.

'If you don't mind I'd like you to take me up by the back stairs, and tell me as we pass where you were standing when you heard Mr Treburyan's voice on the afternoon of his disappearance.'

She led the way towards the servants' quarters. A cupboard-like door gave entrance to the smaller staircase which was steep and straight. She led the way, and halted about half-way up.

'Here,' she said.

He thanked her, and they continued the ascent. A door at the top opened into a corridor. She paused before the first door on the left and flung it open.

'This is the room,' she said.

The room was of a queer shape, the wall on the left being far out of the parallel with the one opposite. It was panelled in dark oak, and the four-poster bed and heavy furniture was at least as old as the room.

'Drake is supposed to have slept here, and in that very bed,' said the girl. 'The man who built the house was one of his captains. Look.' She indicated the fireplace, which was beautifully carved out of the same oak as the panels. In the middle was a shield of arms, and below the name Richard Treburyan, and the date 1572.

Scarpe stood still for a few moments looking around the room. At the foot of the four-poster he noticed his Gladstone and suit-case.

'Of course,' he said, 'this is my room. I think, if you don't mind, now I'm here, I'll try to tidy myself a little.'

She took the hint at once and prepared to withdraw.

'If there is anything you should want,' she said, 'please ring for it. Does this mean that you won't be down again before dinner? Dinner is at half-past seven.'

'I don't think,' he answered, 'that I shall be very long. True, I want to look round a little by myself, but I don't think I shall find much to do until bedtime.'

She left him then, and saw nothing more of him until he appeared in the drawing-room, looking very satisfied with himself, at twenty minutes past seven. There he was introduced to the rather faded kinswoman of Miss Treburyan, of whom, however, he asked no questions concerning the mysterious affair, which was not so much as mentioned at dinner.

Afterwards, in response to a hint from Sylvia, he said, 'I don't want to raise false hopes, but it is almost as good as solved. I hope by tomorrow morning to have some very definite news for you '

The two ladies excused themselves early and retired, and Scarpe sat turning over the pages of books until eleven o'clock, when he turned out the lights, sought his candle in the hall, and made his way up to his panelled room.

Once there he prepared himself for rest, but not for sleep. He stripped back all the heavy curtains that surrounded the bed, exchanged his evening coat for a Norfolk jacket, kicked off his shoes, then lay down on the bed and wrapped a travelling rug around himself. Being thus settled comfortably and having seen that his electric torch was within reach, he blew out the candle.

Outside it was cloudy and there was no moon, but a dim bluish light struggled through the windows and gleamed in little focuses on the polished surfaces of the heavy furniture and the panelled walls. The bedposts loomed up large and gaunt, and to one with unsteady nerves must soon have taken to themselves fantastic shapes and stealthy movement.

Scarpe, however, blessed with a perfect nervous system, lay watching, as calm and alert as if he were a spectator at a cricket match. The whole atmosphere of the room was charged with a vague dread which drifted about him like an invisible mist, and never touched him. Half-an-hour passed, and the watcher on the bed had hardly stirred nor blinked an eye.

The corner of a curtain, caught in a draught from the open window, waved to and fro, and thus set in motion innumerable small shadows which danced back and forth patches of wan light.

How long he had laid there Scarpe could scarcely have told when suddenly he became conscious of some change taking place in the room. It was as if a long panel of light had risen up from the floor and stood perpendicular. He held his breath, waited, and saw it slowly take the shape of a man.

As one by one the features revealed themselves, Scarpe saw that the man was old, and that the face was wrung as if by a sharp pain. The thing raised two shadowy hands and pressed them to its chest, as if to seek relief in the movement. It looked at Scarpe, and its eyes were full of sorrow and appeal. Scarpe met the gaze with grave sympathy, and without fear. Very slightly he inclined his head, as if he understood. Then the wraith turned and glided to the wall opposite the foot of the bed. Then it seemed to linger there a long moment, looking back.

Scarpe leapt out of bed and sprang towards it. It was gone in the flash of a thought, but Scarpe, leaping upon the spot where it had disappeared, began feverishly to feel the panels. A little knot of wood protruded, and against it he pressed his thumb. There was a sharp sound like a single tick of a great clock, and a door in the panels, hitherto invisible, swung open in his face. Exultantly Scarpe turned, and, crossing the room to the nearest chair, seized it and placed it in the doorway to prevent the panels from closing.

Then he stepped into the aperture, flashing his electric torch.

He found himself at the head of a steep and narrow spiral staircase, down which he began to proceed with extreme caution. He had not gone very far when the rays of his torch suddenly focussed themselves upon a tumbled heap—the body of a man lying face downwards upon the stairs.

He turned at once and retraced his steps. There was nothing more to be done that night. He had found the body of Peter Treburyan.

'My dear Miss Treburyan,' he said on the following afternoon, 'you have very little to thank me for, and the affair was really not so difficult as you pay me the compliment to assume.

'What interested me first of all was your uncle's bedroom. Why was it supposed to be haunted in the old days, when nobody had ever seen or heard anything there? Perhaps to keep people from prying about that particular room, I thought. Then you told me that your ancestors were smugglers, and it was very usual for such people to have secret hiding-places for their booty, and sometimes underground passages connected with caves into which contraband cargoes could be hauled from the beach. I thought it likely that you had some such place here, but I was surprised that you knew nothing about it or made no mention of it. Then you mentioned your reformed ancestor, and that explained matters, for such a man might easily let the secret die with him. I decided, if you had such a secret passage, that the entrance was probably in your uncle's bedroom, since that was the room your people in the old days gave out to be haunted, so as perhaps to scare servants and those not in the secret. In that case, since your uncle slept there, he was more likely than anybody else to discover it.

'Once having got as far as that, everything else you told me supported my theory. He was seen that afternoon on a ledge of the cliffs, which, apparently, no man could reach without wings. When you told me that he suffered with his heart, I had no longer the least doubt of the tragedy which we find did actually happen to him.

'He discovered the secret hiding-place and went to explore, finding that it led him right through the house, under the cellars, and right out to a cave high up in the cliff. On his return he found he had shut himself in, for the secret door cannot be opened from the inside. His position was not desperate, for, sooner or later, he must attract attention, but he was a very nervous man, and possibly the prospect of spending an indefinite time in that place in the dark conduced to the heart attack which brought about his death.

I told you yesterday, you will remember, that it was his living voice you heard crying out in pain and distress.

'Having made up my mind that I was right in all this, I only needed to see the apparition of the late Mr Treburyan in the hope that it would show me the exact whereabouts of the secret door. That, I am thankful to say, is just exactly what did happen, and the rest I think you know. What concerned your uncle was your terrible anxiety to know exactly what had become of him, and that anxiety he was continually seeking to relieve in the only way possible to him.'

Nobody's House

They faced each other across the threshold of the great door in the dimness of two meagre lights. It was just dusk on a windy autumn evening, and Mrs Park, the caretaker, had brought a candle with her to answer the summons at the door. Behind the stranger the last grey light of the day filtered through veils of dingy, low-flying clouds. Between them the candle flame fluttered in the draught like a yellow pennon, the cavernous darkness of the hall advancing and retreating like some monster at once curious and shy.

The man was tall and broad and seemingly in the early fifties. He wore a grey moustache and beard, both closely trimmed, and his black velour hat was pulled low down over a high forehead. His overcoat was cut to an old-fashioned pattern, having a cape to it, and it was perhaps this which lent him an air of—even at his years—having outlived his age.

He was fumbling in an inside pocket when the door was opened, and he said nothing until he had produced an envelope.

'I have an order from Messrs Flake and Limpenny to see the house.'

Here he offered Mrs Park the envelope. 'I am afraid I have called at an inopportune time, but I missed one train and the next arrived late. Perhaps, however, you won't mind showing me over?'

He spoke slowly and a little nervously, as if he were repeating a speech which he had previously prepared. His voice was very low and mellowed and gentle. Mrs Park stood back from the threshold.

'Will you come in, sir?' she said. 'I am afraid you won't be seeing the house at its best. I shall have to show you over by candle; there is no gas or electric light.'

He stepped inside and scrutinized her. She was a tall, gaunt, middle-aged woman of the kind which is generally described as 'superior'. Nature had intended her to become matron of an institute. Fate and widowhood had forced her a rung or two down the ladder. She looked what she was—honest, hard-working, and almost devoid of sympathy.

'I'm afraid,' she added in her hard, toneless voice, 'you'll find everything just anyhow. I wasn't expecting anybody. Very few people come here nowadays. And a place of this size takes more than one pair of hands to keep it clean. '

'It has been empty a long time, then?' he hazarded.

'Ever since -' She checked herself suddenly. 'For more than twenty years, I should think.' She turned her shoulder upon him, lifting the candle above her head. 'This is supposed to be a fine hall, and everybody admires the staircase. If the house doesn't find a tenant or a purchaser soon, I hear they intend removing the staircase and selling it separately. There is a lot of fine oak panelling, too. The library'

Turning to see if he were listening, she saw him start and shiver and rub his long, thin hands together.

'Excuse me,' he said. 'I have been a long time in the train, and I am very cold. I wonder if it would be troubling you too much to get me a cup of tea.'

'Yes, I could do that,' she answered. 'The kettle is on, for I intended having one myself. Will you come this way? Perhaps you would like a warm by the fire?'

She led the way across the hall and through a baize-covered door at the end. Turning once to see if she were giving him sufficient light, Mrs Park noticed that he walked with a slight limp. He followed her down a short passage, through a great kitchen ruddy with firelight, down another passage, and into a small room intended to be used as a housekeeper's parlour. Here there was warmth, even stuffiness. A paraffin lamp stood burning on a flaming red table-cloth. The room was full of hideous modem cottage furniture, and decorated largely with the portraits of people who ought to have known better than to be photographed. He saw at a glance Mrs Park in some kind of uniform, Mrs Park's mother wearing bustles, Mrs Park's father in stiff Sunday attire and side-whiskers. But a fire burned brightly in the grate, and a kettle on a brass trivet murmured and rattled its lid. This commonplace room, light and hot and over-furnished was at least a relief from the dark passage and the draughty, gloom-ridden hall.

'I'll give you your tea in here, sir, and take mine in the kitchen,' the caretaker said.

'Nonsense. Why should you? Besides, I want to talk. Oh, here's the order to view. You see .... Mr Stephen Royds—that's my name ... to view He was running his thumbnail along the sheet of heavily headed office notepaper. Mrs Park glanced perfunctorily at the typewriting.

So far as she was concerned an order to view was a superfluous formality. She was more interested in this Mr Royds, who, having removed his hat, disclosed a head of sparse iron-grey hair. He spoke like a gentleman, but there was nothing opulent in his appearance. He looked an unlikely purchaser or tenant; but for that matter she had never been able to visualize the sort of person whom the house would suit.

'I'll remove my greatcoat if you don't mind,' he said, while Mrs Park went to a cupboard for another cup and saucer. 'The room is warm.' He laid the coat across the back of a chair. 'Do you live here entirely alone?'

'Yes.'

'Aren't you—nervous?'

She looked up sharply. 'Nervous? What is there to be nervous about?'

'I didn't know. Some people cannot bear loneliness. Can you tell me why the house has been on the market all these years?'

Mrs Park smiled grimly.

'That's easy enough,' she said. 'It's nobody's house.'

'What do you mean—nobody's house?'

'People who can afford to keep up a great house like this generally want land along with it. There isn't any land. People who don't want land can't afford to keep up a house like this. The estate was sold to Major Skirting He's a house of his own. He's let the land and he's been trying to let or sell the house ever since. I've shown hundreds over but nobody's ever thought twice about taking it. '

'Strange. It's a good house. But the land . . . yes, I quite follow you. Whom used it to belong to?'

Mrs Park set the cup and saucer down upon the table with a rattle.

'A gentleman named Harboys,' she said; and suddenly stood rigid, her head a little on one side, in an attitude of listening.

'Do you hear anything?' he asked sharply.

'No. I'll make the tea.'

'I suppose you sometimes fancy you hear things?'

She bent over the kettle, giving him no answer. He waited until the teapot was full and then gently repeated the question.

'Hear things?' she repeated with some show of asperity. 'No. Why should I?'

'I didn't know. These empty old houses

'I'm not one of the fanciful sort, sir. . . . Will you help yourself to milk and sugar?'

She let him see that the talk had veered in a direction contrary to her liking. There was veiled fear in her eyes, and, watching her intently, he could see that she was not impervious to loneliness. Here was a woman who suffered more than she knew. She could bluff her nerves by sheer will-power, but this will-power was steadily losing in the long battle. Mrs Park was afraid of something, and always, in her inner consciousness, fighting against that fear.

'Thank you,' the stranger said, taking the cup and saucer. 'Who was this Harboys? Is he still alive?'

'I couldn't say.'

'Isn't there some story about the house? Didn't something happen here?'

'I don't know.'

'Forgive me. I think you do.'

'There are stories . . . You don't need to listen . . .'

She spoke jerkily. Once more he remarked that look in her eyes.

'Tell me,' he said gently.

'I can't, sir. If Major Skirting knew I told people I should lose my job. He'd think I was trying to prevent people from taking the house.'

'It wouldn't prevent me. Wasn't this Harboys supposed to have shot'

'Ah!' She set cup and saucer down with a rattle. 'Then you've heard something already, sir!'

'A little. You had better tell me all. It will not affect me as a prospective purchaser.'

Mrs Park passed a hand across her forehead.

'I don't like talking about it, sir. You see, I live here all alone. She checked herself suddenly, finding herself about to admit to a second person something which she never confessed even to herself.

'Just so,' Royds said sympathetically. 'And you sometimes hear noises? What noises?'

'Oh, it's imagination,' she said. 'Or the wind. Sometimes the wind sounds like footsteps and voices, and sometimes I seem to hear. ... It may be a loose door somewhere that bangs. '

He leaned forward, his eyes shining with the excitement of some strange fascination.

'You mean you hear a shot fired?' he asked, scarcely above a whisper.

Her one hand resting on the table-cloth contracted nervously.

'I've known it sound like a shot. Oh, I don't believe. . . .'

'They say the house is haunted?' he asked eagerly.

'They say. . . . Oh, when there's been a tragedy happen in a house people will always'

'Never mind what people say. What do you say?' The timbre of his voice had changed; under excitement it had hardened, grown louder. 'Is the house haunted?'

There was something compelling in Royds' gaze, in the new tone of his voice. She answered him sullenly, helplessly.

'I don't know. I've heard things. I tell myself they're nothing.' She groped for a handkerchief. 'I've got to tell myself they're nothing.'

'You haven't—seen anything?' he asked in a low, strained voice.

'No, thank God! I never go near the library after dark.'

'The library? So it was there. Tell me.'

Mrs Park gulped some tea and replenished her cup with a shaking hand.

'It must have been about twenty years ago,' she said in a low and curiously unwilling tone. 'The place belonged to Mr Gerald Harboys. He was quite young—not much more than thirty, and very well liked. Some said he was a bit queer, but there was a strain of queerness in all the Harboys. Mad on hunting he was, and one of the best riders in these parts. You'll be surprised at the size of the stables when you see them. He had them built.

'He'd married a young wife, one of the Miss Greys from Homfield Manor, and some say he thought more of her than he did of his horses. She used to ride too, and the pair of them, and Mr Peter Marsh from Brinkchurch were always together. Harboys and Marsh had known each other since they were in the cradle. Whether there was really anything between Marsh and Mrs Harboys, I don't know. There's been arguments about that for years, but they're both dead and gone now, and nobody will ever know.

'About one Christmastime Harboys took a fall in the hunting-field and broke his leg, and it was during his convalescence that he got into one of his queer moods. I daresay it was being kept out of the hunting-field which brought it on. His leg mended slowly, and right at the end of January he could only just get about with a stick. Mrs Harboys followed the hounds every time there was a meet in the neighbourhood and, with her husband unable to get about, she saw more of Peter Marsh than usual. But nobody seemed to know that Mr Harboys was jealous or that he suspected anything wrong.

'Well, one day at the end of January, Mrs Harboys went out hunting, and her husband brooded all day over the library fire. During the afternoon he amused himself by cleaning a revolver, which he afterwards laid aside on the mantelpiece within reach. Mrs Harboys came in just after dark. Peter Marsh had been piloting her, and she brought him with her. While she was ordering tea and poached eggs to be sent up to the morning-room, she sent Peter Marsh into the library to get himself a whisky and tell Mr Harboys about the day's hunting. He had not been in the library a minute when angry voices were heard and then a shot. The butler then burst into the room and found Peter Marsh lying dead, and Mr Harboys, still in his chair before the fire, staring wildly at the body, with the revolver in his hand.'

She paused, and in the silence she heard Royds breathing heavily. His head was bent and his gaze lowered to the near edge of the table, so that she could scarcely see his face.

'Mr Harboys,' she resumed, 'pleaded Not Guilty at the trial and said that his mind was a blank at the time when the shot was fired. He couldn't remember anything that had happened between Marsh coming into the room and then the butler bending over the dead body. His counsel put in a plea for insanity, but the jury would not have it. They found him Guilty and added a recommendation to mercy. The death penalty was changed to penal servitude for life.'

She broke off and began to muse, knitting her brows.

'That must be twenty years ago. . . . They let them out after twenty years. He's out already, or soon will be, if he's alive.'

Slowly Royds lifted his head and turned burning eyes upon her face.

'And do you think Harboys did it?' he demanded.

The question took Mrs Park aback.

'Of course! Why! How else could it have happened? There was only those two in the room. It couldn't have happened any other way.'

Royds got upon his legs. His pale face was shining with little drops of moisture, his eyes aflame with a strange passion.

'I swear to you,' he cried, 'that I don't believe Harboys did it. I knew the man'

Mrs Park's stare intensified and she uttered a smothered exclamation.

'I knew him well as child and boy and man. I was at school with Harboys. I tell you he was incapable of murder! All the circumstantial evidence in the world would not weigh an atom with me against my knowledge of his character. They say he had fits of madness. Another lie! But mad or sane he couldn't have done it. He loved his wife—and old Peter Marsh. He knew that they were two of God's best and whitest people. I tell you'

He broke off suddenly and lowered his voice.

'I'm frightening you,' he said. 'I didn't mean to. Oh, but think! There's Harboys been rotting in prison these twenty years, remembering nothing of those few dreadful moments. To this day he doesn't know if he's innocent or guilty. Think of it.'

Mrs Park lifted her white face and twitching lips. One hand had stolen to the region of her heart. Each rapid stroke of her pulses seemed to shake her.

'Why have you come here?' she cried in a voice which rose high and querulous with a nameless dread. 'You don't want the house! You never intended'

'No,' said Royds, 'I came here to find out.'

'What?'

'They say strange things happen in the library. I have heard stories. You tell me you have heard footfalls, voices, the sound of a shot. Don't you understand, woman? What happened in the library that evening twenty years ago is known only to God! The man who lives remembers nothing. If it be true that Peter Marsh returns. . . . Oh, don't you understand? It is the only way of learning ... the only way. . . .'

Mrs Park stood up; her slim body made a barrier between him and the door.

'I can't let you go to the library,' she cried, sharply.

'I must. I'm going to spend the night there. I'm going to wait until Peter'

'I can't let you,' she said again.

'But you must. Don't you understand? This means life or death to a man.'

She backed almost to the door.

'It's madness!' she cried. 'Nobody has ever endured that room after nightfall.'

'I will!'

'I shall be sent away if it is found out.'

'It won't be found out. I'll recompense you if it is. Here, I came prepared to pay for the privilege.' He tugged a bundle of bank notes roughly out of his breast pocket and flung them on the table. 'How much do you want? Five pounds? Ten? Twenty?'

Mrs Park's gaze lingered on the roll of notes. She knew the value of money. Besides, she was alone in the great house with a man whom it might be dangerous to thwart.

'Come,' said Royds, 'here are five five-pound notes. Take them and act like a sensible woman. Then I shall go to the library, and you will make me a fire. Is there any furniture there?'

'No,' muttered the woman, her gaze still on the roll of banknotes.

'Then, if you will permit me, I will take a chair.'

He picked up the notes again and transferred all of them but five to his breast pocket. With these five he advanced and pressed them into the Woman's hand. Her fingers closed over them.

'I'm doing wrong,' she muttered.

'You're doing right. I'll get the truth tonight if I have to summon the devil himself. Now come and help me make a fire in the library'.'

She turned heavily away without a word and went to a cupboard, from the bottom of which she took a bundle of firewood and an old sheet of newspaper, which she dropped on top of the contents of the half-filled scuttle. Then she lit a candle in a brass stick and motioned him towards the door. He picked up a chair as he followed her.

The house was very still as they passed through the kitchen and passages leading to the hall. Their footfalls on the uncarpeted floors rang out sonorously through the hollow shell of the house. To the woman this shattering of a silence which seemed almost sacred was a new weapon put into the hands of Terror. Her overstrained nerves cried out in protest at each of the man's heavy steps. Around her, in the shifting penumbra beyond reach of the candle light, above her in the empty upper chambers of the house, all manner of sleeping horrors, shapeless abominations of the night-world, seemed to waken and listen and draw her. The silent house seemed full of stealthy movement, and each blotch of darkness was an ambush, peopled by the lewd phantasms of her mind. The man walking behind her seemed to be without nerves, or he had so stimulated them as to bring them entirely under his control.

Evidently he knew the house, for he passed her in the hall taking the lead in the procession of two, and went straight to the library door, which he flung open and passed on the crest of the following candlelight.

The library was a long room in an angle of the house. A long row of windows fronted the hearth, and two more faced the door 'The walls were of oak panels stained a mahogany colour, but in that dim light they looked black, as if they were hung with funereal trappings.

The man lingered between the door and the first of the windows while Mrs Park, half closing her eyes, hurried across to the fireplace with the scuttle. He seemed to be searching for something. Presently he found it.

'There's a hole in one of these panels,' he announced.

Mrs Park's heart gave a leap.

'Yes,' she stammered. 'It's a—a bullet hole. The shot lodged there after—after'

'Yes,' he said quietly, 'I understand.' He crossed the room with a chair and set it down at that comer of the hearth which faced the door and the damaged panel. 'And that afternoon, over twenty years ago, I was sitting here'

There was a crash as the scuttle fell from the woman's hands. All her horror and amazement expressed itself in one thin, muffled scream.

'You were sitting there! You! Gerald Harboys! Gerald Harboys, the murderer!'

He answered quietly, 'Gerald Harboys or Stephen Royds—God help me, what does it matter? Murderer or not—only God knows! But I shall learn tonight. Light that fire, woman, and then leave me. '

She left him and stumbled blindly back to the little vulgar room behind the kitchen. But a fascination stronger than terror drew her back to the outside of the library door, there tremblingly to wait and to listen. . . . Harboys, to give him his real name at the last, settled himself on the chair, and at first busied himself with the building up of the fire. Then he took a revolver from his coat pocket, and placed it upon the mantelpiece within his reach. This done he looked out across the room with a steady gaze.

The firelight wrought strange patterns among the shadows, but in the swiftly changing measures of this shadow-dance he found nothing of what he sought. Presently he began to speak aloud, quietly but very distinctly, so that the shivering woman outside the door brought her hands to her tightening throat.

'Peter, Peter.' The tone was almost wheedling. 'Can you hear me? I'm sitting in just the same place that I sat that evening, with my bad leg resting on a stool. Here am I, and here's that damned revolver. Now, Peter, won't you come? They say you're always here—that you can't rest because your best friend shot you. Did I shoot you, Peter? My mind's a blank—a blank! For twenty years I have been trying to remember. I have not known peace day and night for twenty years, Peter. Oh, come and tell me! I want to know—to know. There's something wrong, Peter. I couldn't have done it. How could I have shot you, boy?'

He relapsed into silence, his gaze never leaving the space between the door and the first window. After a long minute his voice broke out again, choked and almost tearful.

'Is it because you hate me that you won't show yourself, Peter? Was I mad? and did I do it after all? Don't hate me, Peter. I've suffered! Have pity!

One way or another I want to end this agony tonight. Oh, God, make him merciful to me! Peter, we'd been friends so long. School . . . don't you remember Wryvem, and those long talks under the lime-trees in the Close on summer nights? And study teas? And going up to Lord's?'

He babbled on, while kaleidoscopic pictures passed before the eyes of his memory. Cool, dewy morning, and the cricket eleven tumbling out of houses for fielding practice; rows of languid boys in dim classrooms and a scratching of pens; bright sunlight, and white shapes moving on a green sward; crowded touch-lines, and the scrum forming, and goal-posts standing up stark against a grey November sky. In each and all of them he caught a wavering, vanishing glimpse of Peter Marsh.

'Peter!' he cried out again. 'Can't you hear me? Won't you come to me?

You do come back. They all say so. That woman hears you. You—in your scarlet coat, as you came in that evening. I remember . . . when I saw you lying there . . . the blood scarcely showed. I was sitting her waiting for Muriel. I heard you both come up the drive. Muriel was laughing at something. You were both talking to the groom outside. Then I heard you in the hall, and Muriel ordered tea and went upstairs. And I thought, "She doesn't come in to see me. I'm nothing to her now I'm crocked. It's all Peter, Peter, Peter. By God!" I said, "I've been blind as well as lame. The things I've seen which they pretended were nothing. . . . The things I haven't seen, but heard of in whispers and hints." All in a moment my brain caught fire. "Damn you!" I said, "I'll teach you to make a cuckold of a lame man!"

Then ….you came in.'

The trembling woman outside heard him utter a hoarse cry.

'Peter! Peter! Oh, God, I'm beginning to remember. You stood where you're standing now, touching the handle of the door. That's right! And you said—I remember now—"Give us a peg, Jerry. I'm frozen. There's a devil of an east wind." Peter! Peter! Don't look like that! I'm remembering . . . Oh, God, have mercy . . . have mercy!'

A hoarse scream echoed through the room, a chair heeled over with a crash, and then followed a frenzied shouting.

'I remember ... I remember . . . damn you! when you turned your back on me . . . like that –'

A shot rang out; then another. Then silence enfolded Nobody's House, and its one living inmate, a swooning woman, who clung to the oak balustrade.

It was half-an-hour later when Mrs Park forced herself to enter the library. The red glow of the fire was still dancing on the walls and floor. For a moment one ruddy gleam seemed to take a fantastic shape—like the prostrate figure of a man in hunting pink.

Harboys lay crumpled and face downwards across the hearth, the revolver still in his hand, the ugly wound in his temple mercifully hidden. To that end had he remembered.

Where there had been a bullet hole in one of the panels, the police next morning found two. They were side by side and scarcely an inch apart.

The Yellow Curtains

I

I used to see a great deal of the Denveys in those good days. Their house, five miles away, provided me with an occasional glimpse of home life, so grateful and sometimes so necessary to a boy segregated among his own kind for three months on end at boarding school. Geoffrey Denvey and I were in the same Form at Huxminster, where he was an envied—and therefore despised—day-boy, who cycled back every evening to a real home, leaving us others to the Spartan amenities of our respective boarding-houses. Geoffrey often asked me over to his place on Sundays and on half holidays when it was possible to escape compulsory games. We were great friends, although the friendship on my side owed something to my unconfessed admiration for his sister Myra. It was partly on her account that I angled for, and gladly accepted, invitations to Alma Lawn, and it was she who inspired all my precocious dreams when I was seventeen.

It was a small house, and there was nothing at all luxurious about it, but it was the best home I have ever known. Mrs Denvey hadn't much money, and more than half her income must have gone on the education of the three children. But she had the great gift of making everybody about her happy, she was so jolly, and sympathetic and broadminded, such an ideal 'mater'.

Besides Mrs Denvey and Geoffrey and Myra the household included Olive and Martha. Martha was the one maid of the establishment, an elderly gloomy woman, whose permanent expression suggested chronic toothache and whose normal tone of voice was a deep growl. Her aggressive taciturnity was one of the many household jokes, and her faithfulness and loyal service were numbered among the many household blessings.

Olive was fifteen then, and she had been adopted by Mrs Denvey as a daughter, and by the Denvey children as a sister. She was orphaned and nearly penniless, a very distant connection of the Denveys, and she had found her way into a heart large enough to mother all the children in Christendom She was small and dark, with grey, far-seeing eyes, whereas Geoffrey and Myra were both fair.

From our point of view, the greatest charm of the place was the gardener's cottage at the end of the garden. It stood, like the house, flush with the road, with the length of the garden between. When Mrs Denvey took Alma Lawn, she found herself with an empty gardener's cottage, and no gardener to put in it, since she could afford only an odd-job man once or twice a week. Those were the days when there was no shortage of cottages, its rentable value was not more than two shillings a week; and Mrs Denvey did not wish to have a family of villagers living in her own garden. It was thus left empty and the children 'bagged' it. 'This,' they said, 'is ours', and they proceeded to furnish it.

Every broken chair, every box capable of being sat on, every scrap of discarded carpet and every chipped vase found its way into the cottage. Olive and the young Denveys always spoke of it as their house and spent most of their playtime there. With the perversity of children they preferred it to the civilized establishment at the other end of the garden.

Mrs Denvey played the game, as only she could. She never entered the cottage except by invitation. On ceremonial occasions, heartily disliked by Martha because of the exigencies of transport, she would be asked there to tea, when she always gave a delightfully absurd imitation of the polite visitor who was almost a stranger, and gravely discussed with Myra and Olive the servant problem and the cost of living. To add to the entertainment, the broken chair on which she sat always collapsed sooner or later, and her affected embarrassment and frenzied apologies for having broken the beautiful furniture were a sheer delight. Invariably ongoing she 'left cards' in a broken saucer on the window-ledge, these cards having been previously abstracted from packets of her favourite brand of cigarettes.

Occasionally Geoffrey invited Frobisher besides myself. Frobisher was in our form and in my House, and he took some pains to cultivate Geoffrey. His method consisted mainly of being host at expensive feasts, and an occasional invitation to Alma Lawn was Geoffrey's only means of returning these hospitalities. He was a nice enough boy, but none of us liked him very much.

He was a little too flamboyant for our simplicities. His father was a Conservative M.P., and he lived in a ring park in the midst of six thousand of his own acres. He was given to mentioning these things, although I verily believe there was nothing of the snob about him; but he made an odd number, and we felt him to be out of place in a household which contained neither butler nor footman.

Certainly Frobisher did not fit in to the cottage, where—particularly on wet afternoons—we sometimes lit fires and cooked godless messes. The chimneys, which had not been swept within living memory, invariably rejected the smoke, and these experiments nearly always ended in our being driven out into the fresh air, grimy and feeling like half-cured hams, but still laughing and happy.

There was a tacit understanding between the four of us. If we walked a hundred yards Geoffrey paired with Olive and I with Myra, unless Frobisher happened to be with us, when the two girls were left to keep each other company. This was not Frobisher's fault; it was all due to Geoffrey and me. It amuses me to look back and remember how jealous we both were of him. Gala times were the mid-term weekends which I always spent with the Denveys. Frobisher never came; he went home to the Ancestral Mansion, as we always called it. Then, besides three long days were two delightful evenings, when Mrs Denvey had not to study the clock and say to me, 'I don't want to hurry you, Frank, but you know what your housemaster said about punctuality, and I don't want to stop you from coming again.'

On one of those long weekends, the Whitsuntide of 1913, I kept my eighteenth birthday. In celebration a cake was made and cooked over a hay-fire in the cottage on Sunday afternoon. It smelled horrid and tasted even worse, and presently the heat and the smoke drove us forth into the fresh air of the garden. We lay propped at all angles on the grass and Geoffrey produced contraband cigarettes and handed them round.

'You know,' he said thoughtfully, 'it could be made very nice.'

'What, that filthy cake?' I demanded.

'I told him,' said Myra, 'you can't make cake properly in a saucepan.'

'Still,' said Geoffrey, 'it wouldn't have turned out like bad glue if you'd let me mix it properly. But I wasn't talking about that; I was talking about the cottage itself. Olive and I are going to live in it when we're married.'

The remark seemed to me all the funnier because it was uttered with such an air of seriousness. Myra and I both laughed and looked at Olive. She, too, remained quite serious and matter-of-fact, except that her eyes, as we used to tell her, seemed to be looking at the day after tomorrow.

'Well, I hope you'll have the chimneys swept first,' I said.

'Oh, that's nothing. We're going to have those two rooms knocked into one, and make a big lounge. And we'll have yellow curtains in the windows, and a fawn carpet'

'And peacock-blue cushions and chair covers,' said Olive.

'And a big dresser full of blue china.'

'And lots of bright brass ornaments for the mantelpiece.'

I rolled over and laughed.

'What about the larder?' I asked. 'What are you going to have in that?'

'He means,' Myra explained obligingly, 'how are you going to live? Not many jobs going around here, you know. And not being a bloated aristocrat like Frobisher, you'll have to focus your massive intellect on making a living.'

Geoffrey waved his cigarette airily.

'We shan't want much,' he said.

'Just as well, dears,' said Myra, showing the tip of her tongue. 'You won't be disappointed then, will you?'

'I think I shall be an artist,' Geoffrey explained. 'Crawford says my figure drawing isn't half bad, and I should have quite a chance if I took it up seriously. And artists can live where they dam well please.'

It began to dawn on me that Geoffrey was really serious.

I was a year older, and, therefore, old enough to be amused. But I was glad, too, because this would give me, as soon as I could summon the nerve, an excuse for suggesting some similar romantic arrangement to Myra. That, however, I was never quite able to do, because I was secretly shy and sorely afraid of her.

That same night, when our belated bedtime was drawing near, Geoffrey characteristically told his mother of his idyllic intentions. He struck a preposterous attitude, leaning his right arm on one of Olive's shoulders, and raising and waggling his left heel.

'I suppose you know, mater,' he drawled, 'that we're enga-a-ged?'

'Oh!' said Mrs Denvey, and her mouth was ominous while her eyes twinkled.

'And we're going to live in the cottage,' he proceeded, 'and knock those two rooms into one. And we'll have yellow curtains in the windows, and a fawn carpet, and peacock-blue'

'You'd better wait until you're too old to be spanked,' said Mrs Denvey, 'before you talk to me about getting married.'

'Boo to you,' said Geoffrey pleasantly. 'In fact, two boos!'

He dodged behind Olive as his mother laughingly made a dive for him.

'And what's to become of the poor old mater?' she demanded.

'Oh, you'll go on living here, and have us close handy for company.

We'll be the poor at your gate. You'll be Mrs Dives, and we'll be Mr and Mrs Lazarus. '

'I think,' I said, pretending to joke, 'I'd better marry Myra and come and live with you, Mrs Denvey. Much more comfortable here than the cottage.'

Instantly she turned her simulated wrath upon me.

'Don't you talk to me about marrying Myra, you preposterous brat!' she exclaimed. 'I don't know what children are coming to nowadays.'

But all the while there was laughter and kindness in her eyes, and I knew that she regarded us as so many nice babies who really needed no looking after. She shooed us all to the door as if she were driving a flock of geese.

'Out with you!' she cried. 'One breath of fresh air in the garden before bed, and no more nonsense.'

Geoffrey crooked his arm for Olive to take.

'Come on, missus,' he said; and he looked back over his shoulder at his mother, and laughed.

Myra and I followed them out into a clear night of stars, a delicious night which smelled of cattle and flowers, and hay and duck-ponds; and side by side we began to pace the lawn, keeping our distance from the other two.

'You know,' said Myra in a low voice, 'Olive and Geoffrey are quite serious, or they think they are.'

'Awful rot, at their age!' said I, fishing.

'Of course!' Myra agreed, declining the bait.

But I think the four of us were quite confident that our dreams would come true. We saw our future quite clearly, as a cheating Sybil might have seen it for us in the crystal.

Geoffrey tackled me next morning.

'I say,' he remarked awkwardly, 'no telling the other chaps about Olive and me and—and the cottage, you know.'

'My dear chap,' I said, rather annoyed, 'I don't blab about what happens here.'

Frobisher came over once or twice before the end of the term, learned of the cottage's new destiny, and was sworn to secrecy. He was tolerant about it and a little patronising. He, it appeared, would be expected to marry into the county and live in a state of magnificence which, he alleged, would be rather a bore.

Next year Geoffrey and I both left school—about ten days before the outbreak of war.

II

In the dawn of an autumn morning in 1917, Geoffrey Denvey, lieutenant and acting-captain, stood leaning an elbow on the mud of a fire-step, waiting for zero hour.

The coming attack had been well advertised by the preliminary barrage which was still in progress. Behind, field guns and howitzers were barking and thundering. High overhead the air seemed full of the rushing of invisible trains, and the screaming of whirlwinds. Evidently the enemy resented this treatment, for he was retaliating with spirit. The trench, as Geoffrey remarked to his batman, was 'no place for a clergyman's son'. The crescendo shrieks of enemy shells joined in the din, and this way and that huge geysers of black earth arose, melting away so slowly that they seemed to hang still on the air. Earth and stones descended in gusty showers on the men who stood fidgeting, with their bayonets already fixed, straining their ears for the sharp note of a whistle.

It came at last. Geoffrey dropped the whistle from his mouth, climbed on to the fire-step, hoisted himself over, and stood looking around him as the heads and shoulders of men encumbered with rifles, bombs, shovels, and all the paraphernalia of storm troops appeared above the parapet. They came slowly, scrambling first upon their knees and then rising stiffly. Geoffrey waved frantically to them not to bunch, and section commanders hurried hither and thither, barking like sheep-dogs.

The ragged line moved. Out in front, in the middle distance, was a haze of flying debris, sparkling with quick flashes, where black columns of flung earth melted into grey. The heavy rattling of machine-guns and the staccato cracking of rifles mingled with the din. The air was lashed as with whips and the swift winnowing of wings.

Geoffrey threaded his way between a maze of fresh shell-holes which still reeked of explosive, and turned to look at his men. Good to have men to look after, they kept one from thinking of other things. They picked their way slowly, most of them with heads slightly bent, bowed down by their burdens. Nearly all were smoking, some were muttering to themselves, but most faces were apathetic. A few flinched and ducked as flaming whizz-bangs rushed to earth behind them. But for the most part they reminded him of nothing so much as tired workmen plodding home through a shower of rain. Could anything in this world be so unlike a bayonet charge as the thing itself?

'Steady, you chaps!'

He talked to them, although they could not hear. They were getting too far ahead of A Company on the right, and he signalled to them to lie down.

Not so bad, so far. Funny how anything came to be left alive in this storm of bullets.

Up again. His batman half rose, dropped face downwards once more, and lay still. They'd got the range now. A shrapnel helmet spun in the air like a coin, and the man who had worn it sagged and fell like a half empty sack. Men began to jump and start as if stung, and sink down, or stagger on with their backs hunched and a hand pressed to an arm or a leg. Some of the wounded were dropping into shell holes, others crawling back.

Something like a hot iron seared Geoffrey's forehead. He pressed his knuckles to it and found a broad red stain on the back of his hand.

That was near!

'Come on you chaps!'

If only our gunners had found their blasted machine-gun emplacements. . . . This was very strange! Where was he? Everything had gone queer, become suddenly unreal. Mustn't lie here . . . but . . . but . . . No, it didn't hurt very much . . . unless he moved. . . .

Dimly he heard in the near distance shouts, yells, and the staccato explosions of bombs. Our men were in among them. Heavy footfalls plodded past him. That was the second wave coming over. But it was all only a dream. Nothing was real except Olive, and the mater, and the cottage, and Myra, and Frank. Across the years he heard the tinkling of the tea-bell from the open french windows of Alma Lawn. . . .

An hour later two stretcher-bearers found him. One of them bent over him and then shook his head at the other. They had no time to waste on any who were beyond human aid But hearing a murmur the man bent to listen, and unhitching Geoffrey's water-bottle, he held it to his lips.

'Wot was he saying?' asked the other presently.

'Something about furniture—yellow curtains and what not.'

'Well, I'm ----!' remarked the second stretcher-bearer, making use of the private soldier's favourite past participle.

III

Mrs Denvey did not long survive Geoffrey. I came home on leave in February '18 to find Myra working on the land. Olive was scrubbing a hospital somewhere in Cheltenham. Our knowledge that the 'old firm' was broken up forever drew us closer together. It was not a long engagement.

We were married on the tenth of my fourteen days' leave. In the spring of 1919 I found myself back in civilian clothes once more, master of a seven-roomed suburban villa, with a job in the City, a young wife, and the prospect of a happy humdrum future.

It took time to settle down. The War had shaken us all like a severe illness. The changes in our lives had been all too violent. Five years since we had been children, and although youth had been knocked out of us we were little more than children now.

I had passed Alma Lawn once in a friend's car, and it took me like a blow over the heart to see an alien look about the house and unfamiliar blinds in the windows. And the cottage was gone altogether. The new owner had had it pulled down to make way for a hideous wooden garage. I did not even know the new owner's name, but I hated him for having done it. At twenty-four I already began to understand why old people resent changes.

The truth is that Myra and I were in danger of lapsing into a settled melancholy. We had an unexpressed grudge against Providence for shattering our dreams and foiling all our hopes. We had each other, but somehow we weren't quite complete without Geoffrey and his mother.

Olive we saw fairly often, but she didn't help much. She looked ten years more than her age and went through life as if the act of living were a distasteful duty. She, too, had a job in London, and lived in South Kensington with some older woman whom she had met while she was doing war-work. Geoffrey's death had soured her to the core, and it was plain that she, too, cherished a grudge.

Sometimes she came down to spend a weekend with us, but she was always a skeleton at feasts which were never so hilarious as to need a sobering influence. Once I heard her dissuading Myra from going to church.

'I never go now,' she said. 'I have something better to do than waste my time in listening to a man who would expect me to believe that I'm someday going to see Geoffrey again!' And she uttered a dreadful derisive laugh which went through me like a knife.

And now comes the first of the really strange things that happened. In March 1920, Olive went down with pneumonia, recovered, and, during her convalescence, became her old self again. I'd heard of people's natures being changed by severe illness, but I wouldn't have believed it in Olive's case. Myra flew to her side to help nurse her during the crisis, and came back after two or three days, when Olive had safely turned the comer, wearing so long a face that I thought the worst had happened.

'It was ghastly!' she murmured, burying her face against my shoulder.

'On Saturday night, when it was touch and go, poor Olive was delirious, and she thought she was married to Geoffrey and living in the cottage at Alma Lawn, as they'd always said they would. I didn't know how to stay in the room with her. She kept pointing out the furniture and the decorations to me.

"Yes," she said, "we always said we'd have yellow curtains, didn't we? Everything's happened just as we said it would." I almost hoped she'd die believing that; she was so happy, poor girl. And then—and then she said, "That scar on Geoffrey's forehead? Yes, it's a wound he got during the War. But it doesn't hurt now, does it, darling?" But, Frank, tell me—Geoffrey wasn't hit in the head, was he?'

'Well,' I answered heavily, 'as a matter of fact he was. It must have been just before he—went down. It wasn't a serious wound, though, it only grazed him.'

I had been very sparing of details of Geoffrey's end, and just then Myra and I must have been pondering the same problem.

'Did you tell Olive?' she asked.

'No, I didn't,' I answered, firmly and truthfully.

'Then how could she have known?'

'Goodness knows!' I answered irritably. For both our sakes I wanted to change the subject.

And the strangest possible sequel followed about seven months later. I was making my way homeward on a chilly, unkind October evening.

Waterloo Station was more crowded than usual, for there had been a race-meeting somewhere down the line, and every two or three minutes special trains were disgorging their crowds of mixed humanity. I cannoned against a magnificent person, who wore binoculars slung on his shoulders and might have stepped straight out of one of those tailors' plates which tell you plainly how a real racing-man ought to look. We exchanged apologies, and then he uttered a queer, high-pitched cry, and addressed me by name. I looked at him again, and he was Frobisher.

Of course, we stood and talked. We hadn't seen each other since our last day at school. He had grown stouter and had mellowed a little, but he was still the same 'Frobby'. He asked me where I was living and I told him. 'Come and have a drink,' he said. 'You've got millions of trains.'

He was voluble and amusing. It seemed that nowadays he owned racehorses, one of which had gained an unexpected victory in a selling plate that afternoon.

We joined the crowd of sandwich-eating, beer-drinking humanity around the curved bar, and tried, for some time in vain, to attract the attention of one of the harassed young women.

'Ever see anything of the old crowd?' he asked, turning to me after he had just failed to place an order.

I thought he was referring to our contemporaries at school, and shook my head.

'I was down there last March,' he rattled on. 'You used to be awfully pally with the Denveys, usen't you? Well, I had rather a joyous surprise. Some ass told me that Geoffrey Denvey was knocked out in the War.'

'So he was,' I said.

It happened that Frobisher did not hear me. He had caught one of the attendants in the act of serving the man on his left, and he turned swiftly to engage her attention.

'Two Scotches and a Schweppes, please. Yes, I've been thinking all along that old Geoffrey had gone west. I was frightfully bucked when I ran across him and Olive. I s'pose you know he married her?'

He looked at my blank face, misread what he saw there, and laughed.

'So you haven't been keeping up with them?' he remarked. 'It's funny how one loses touch without meaning to. The War was such a big bite out of one's life. I ran across Olive and Geoffrey last March. It was the funniest thing in the world how it happened. If you want to know where they're living I can tell you—and you've been in the place hundreds of times. Say when.'

It took my breath away. He might have known that I should not have lost touch with Geoffrey if he'd been alive. It was on my tongue to say, 'Geoffrey was killed three years ago. I was in the same batt. and saw him when he was brought in. Incidentally, I married his sister.' But I didn't say it. The apparently wanton, heartless stupidity of the lie held me dumb. He must have had some reason, I thought, for making such a statement, and I let him go on talking in the hope that he would betray it.

'They're living,' continued Frobisher, with a laugh at once hearty and sentimental, 'in that old cottage in the garden of Alma Lawn, where they used to say they were going to live. The whole thing's almost like a fairy tale.'

Another good lie, I thought grimly. The cottage had been pulled down at least two years since. And again I wondered irritably why he was troubling to tell me such painful nonsense.

'I must tell you about it,' he said, after a sip of whisky. 'I was staying at my Cousin Farley's place, which is only about twenty miles from Huxminster, when I saw in the Sporting Life that the school was playing Blackheath A. That would have been the second Saturday in March. Well, I'd got rather a guilty conscience about never having been near the place since I left, so I borrowed Farley's Singer and drove over after lunch. Blackheath popped it across us, but it was a pretty good game, and, of course, I met crowds of beaks I knew, and one or two lanky louts in the Sixth who were blancoing cricket boots in our last term. Made me feel young to find 'em still there. Well, it all merged into a rather happy evening, and it ended in my sitting down to dinner in plus-fours with the Old Man and the Queen of Spades, neither of whom have altered a day.

'Well, I left 'em about ten o'clock and started to drive back; and I took the Fairstow road because, although it's a bit further round, it's better at night. It wasn't until I was breezing through a village about five miles out that I realized I'd soon be passing the house where the Denveys used to live. I wondered if Mrs Denvey and the girls were still there—some ass had told me that old Geoffrey had gone west—but it was too late to call. And when I passed the house there wasn't a light showing anywhere.

'I'd come down to a crawl to have a good look round in passing, and I hadn't got up any speed when I passed the end of the garden and that old cottage which we used to fool about in. There were lights in the cottage streaming right out across the road, and—it's funny how things come back to you—do you know what made me stop?'

I shook my head, shutting my teeth fast.

'There were yellow curtains in the front windows. And it all came back to me in a flash—how Olive and Geoffrey used to say they were going to furnish the place. When I saw those yellow curtains I knew that it was a hundred to one that at least one of them was living there, so I pulled in sharp and got out. And then I went up to the door and knocked.

'It was old Geoffrey himself who came to the door—what's the matter?—and I thought, "Well, old lad, you can't be killed!" I couldn't see him very clearly, but I knew him at once by his shape. He knew me, too, and asked me in. He was very quiet; quite genial, you know, but not exactly overwhelming. And he didn't seem a bit surprised to see me. He just called out, "Olive, here's Frobisher." And there was Olive sitting in a chair with her back to that window we broke playing hand-ball.'

'This,' I said grimly, 'was the second Saturday in March this year?'

'You're dashed particular about dates,' he laughed. 'That's right. It was the night of the Blackheath match. Why?'

I did not trouble to tell him on that particular night Olive had been lying between life and death in a London lodging. I wanted him to go on to the end.

'You'd hardly know the cottage,' he continued. 'They've turned all the ground floor except the kitchen into one big room, just as they said they were going to, and besides the yellow curtains they'd got their fawn carpet and peacock-blue cushions. But they'd changed a lot. They seemed awfully happy, but happy in a quiet, self-contained sort of way which made me feel rather left out in the cold. Geoffrey wore his old uniform, which seemed rather odd, until it occurred to me that he was probably pretty hard up and meant to wear it out indoors. When I saw him in the light I noticed that he had a white scar right across his forehead . . . Don't jump like that! What's the matter with you, man?

'Well, they didn't seem as elated at seeing me as I wanted them to be, and, for some reason which I can't understand, I was half scared of them. They'd both changed so much. I was just going to sit down when Olive gravely told me that it was mother's chair, as if nobody else ought to sit in it, so I took another pew. And then I began to babble congratulations because they'd got married, and reminded them how they'd planned the decorations of the place when they were kids. And Olive said, "Yes, we always said we'd have yellow curtains, didn't we? Everything's happened just as we said it would." ' He paused to drink.

I felt my brain turn, and, for a moment, the floor seemed to slip from under my feet. In some incalculable fraction of time there flashed into my mind Myra's account of Olive in her delirium—the self-same words uttered on the self-same night. For just a second I had to fight hard to keep my reason, and I clung grotesquely to the fact that I was standing at the buffet on Waterloo Station, and that a cockney clerk standing just behind Frobisher was trying to order coffee. It was a struggle to keep the workaday crowd around me from seeming grotesque figures moving in a dream.

'What's the matter?' Frobisher asked, regarding me anxiously.

'Nothing. I'm only tired.' I was now leaning on the counter. 'Go on.'

'Oh, there's nothing much to tell. I didn't stay long. They'd changed in some queer way which I can't describe, and I wasn't a bit comfortable with them. They were very happy and self-contained and tremendously in love, and that didn't seem to make talking any easier. And when you asked one a question the other generally answered it. For instance, when I asked old Geoffrey how he came by the scar on his forehead, Olive said'

But I already knew what Olive had said, and I leaned heavier on the counter to hear the words which I knew were coming.

'I was glad to have seen 'em again, of course,' Frobisher chattered on,

'but I wasn't sorry to go. In fact, I quite forgot to ask if they had heard anything of you or inquire after Geoffrey's sister—what was her name?—Myra. Do you ever see anything of her, by the way? They've both changed a lot, but then time passes, and one can't expect everything and everybody to remain the same.'

I nodded heavily. So far as I was concerned, nothing would ever be quite the same again.

Did I tell Frobisher? No, I did not. He would not have believed me, and if I had proved to him that he had entered a non-existent cottage and talked to a dead man, to say nothing of a woman who was lying sick a hundred miles away at the time, he would have gone to any extreme rather than face the facts. Besides, it would have troubled him, given his mind uncomfortable thoughts which it was not built to hold, got in the way of his racing and of his golf. . . .

It was my message—our message—not his, although he had brought it.

Had he been meant to understand he would have known all that Saturday night in March. He is happier as he is.

But we three—Myra and Olive and I—we are very certain that whether Frobisher dreamed, imagined, or invented his tale, it is all far beyond the realm of possible coincidence; and for us life and death are no longer the precarious adventures they once seemed.

So I am quite sure that I shall see old Geoffrey again, and perhaps—who knows?—when I have parted from my last breath I shall step straight out of my outworn carcase on to the threshold of the old gardener's cottage, and perhaps see Myra, if she has gone first, smiling at me in greeting between the yellow curtains of an open window.

Between the Minute and the Hour

There is no more commonplace stretch of thoroughfare in the United Kingdom than the London Road at Nesthall between Station Road and Beryl Avenue. A row of small, dingy villas and a row of new and diminutive shops face each other across the tram-lines which stretch between Hammersmith and a distant suburb, once a country town. Nearly all of these shops are for the sale of sweets, tobacco, and newspapers, so that it seems strange that there should be a livelihood in any one of them.

Charles Trimmer kept the fifth shop down, as you would count them with your back to London. His commonplace name appeared above his one commonplace window, with 'Newsagent' on one side of it and 'Tobacconist' on the other. The window displayed an assortment of cheap sweets in bottles and open boxes, picture-postcards in doubtful taste, flies when in season, and dummy packets of tobacco and cigarettes.

Trimmer himself was commonplace in mind and appearance to match his surroundings and his avocation. If I lay particular stress on this, it is because it serves to make this strange narrative the stranger. He was short, turned forty, slightly bald, with a slim, dark, waxed moustache. His hobbies may be said to have consisted of watching professional football—he was a firm 'supporter' of Brentford whenever he could get away—and putting odd shillings on horses which seldom won. As he had only his own mouth to feed, the shop kept him without hardship. He lived alone, but an elderly woman came in daily to cook his dinner and do the rougher housework. For the rest, you must imagine him to be a colourless individual, almost without personality, and with, of course, an atrocious accent, part Cockney and part peculiar to the Middlesex suburbs. Yet to this colourless little man in his squalid surroundings befell an adventure the like of which had never before been dreamed.

It was eight o'clock on a Wednesday evening in March, the end of a gusty, drizzling day without a hint of spring in the air. Trimmer's day's work was nearly over. His cold supper lay awaiting him, and in half an hour he would be free to stroll down to the Station Hotel and drink his usual two half-pints of bitter beer. With a cigarette hanging from his under-lip, he was approaching the shop door, to close it, when two ragged figures entered.

The first was a woman, short, swarthy, grey-haired, and indescribably dirty, with an enormous cast in her left eye which seemed in perpetual contemplation of the bridge of her nose. She was followed by a tall, rickety boy in rags who might have been either her son or her grandson. Trimmer, knowing from experience that these were not likely to be customers, immediately assumed an air of hostility.

'Spare us a copper or a mouthful o' food, kind gentleman!' the woman whined. 'I've got two dear little bybies starvin'

Trimmer made a gesture towards the door.

'''Op it!' he said. 'I've got precious little for myself, let alone for you.'

'I'll give you a wish in exchange, pretty gentleman—a good wish, a wish o' wonderment for you. You wouldn't grudge a bit o' bread for my precious children, pretty gentleman? You'

Trimmer advanced upon her almost threateningly.

'Pop orf!' he cried. 'Did you 'ear what I said? Pop orf!'

The ragged woman drew herself up so that she seemed to grow much taller. She stared at him with an intensity that made him fall back a step as if her very gaze were a concrete thing which had pushed him. She raised her open hands above the level of her shoulders.

'Then may the bitterest curse -'

In a moment the boy had caught one of her hands and was trying to clap his own hand over her mouth.

'Mother, mother,' he cried, 'for God's sake'

Trimmer stared at the pair in something like horror. He did not believe in curses. He had all the materialism of the true Cockney. But the intensity of the woman's manner, the sudden queerness in her eyes for which the cast did not wholly account, and the boy's evident fear worked on his undeveloped imagination.

'All right, missus,' he said, a little surprised at his own soothing tone. 'You don't want to take on like that.'

The intensity of the woman's manner subsided a little.

'A bit o' food for me and my starvin' family. 'T'was all I asked.'

Trimmer persuaded himself that he was sorry for her. He was not essentially ill-natured. Casting about in his mind for something that he could give her without leaving himself the poorer, he bethought him of some biscuits which had gone soft and pappy through having been kept too long in stock. He went to the tin, emptied its contents into a large bag, and handed the bag to the woman.

She took it without thanks, picked out a biscuit, and nibbled at it. He saw the queerness come back into her eyes.

'A strange gift you have given me, master,' she said, 'and a strange gift I give you in return. When night turns to morning, between the minute and the hour is your time.'

Once more the boy seemed disturbed. 'Mother!' he cried, in expostulation.

'I have said what I have said,' she answered. 'The end shall be of his own seeking. Between the minute and the hour!'

With that, slowly, they passed out of the shop. Trimmer, as he locked the door behind them, reflected that it was a 'rum start'. He noticed that his hand trembled as it turned the key.

For no reason that he could translate into the language of his own thoughts the woman's words haunted Trimmer. He denied to himself that he was in any way afraid; he was merely curious as to what meaning might be attached to what she had said. Had she a real thought in her head, or had she been trying to frighten him with meaningless rubbish?

Several days passed and Trimmer, in his leisure, still vexed his mind with the conundrum. He answered it in a half satisfactory manner. When night turned to morning was technically twelve o'clock midnight. After that it was called A.M., which to him meant nothing. Between the minute and the hour! That must mean the minute before midnight. But why was that his time? What had she meant by her vague threat, if, indeed, she had meant anything at all?

Trimmer was generally in bed before eleven and asleep very shortly afterwards, but about ten days later he sat up late in the closed shop, working at his accounts. He was almost done when he glanced up at the little striking clock which he kept on the shelf behind the counter. It wanted just two minutes to the hour of midnight.

Trimmer was not nervous by temperament, but a man sitting up late alone and at work may be excused if he finds himself the victim of strange fancies. In another minute it would be what the old woman had called his time, and once again he asked himself what she had meant by that. Had she meant that he would die at that hour?

He rose and went to the door of the shop, his gaze still on the clock. The upper panels of the door were glass and screened by a green linen blind. Outside he could hear a late tram, moaning on its way to the depot. He was grateful for this friendly sound from the familiar workaday world.

He lifted the curtain and peered through the glass, and then, before his eyes were accustomed to the darkness outside and he could see anything save his own wan reflection, something happened which sent a sudden rush of blood to his heart. The noise of the tram had ceased, and ceased in such a way that the crack of a pistol would have been less startling than this sudden silence. It was not that the tram had suddenly stopped.

Afterwards, fumbling for phrases, he recorded that the sound 'disappeared'. This is a contradiction in terms, but it is sufficiently graphic to serve for what he intended to express.

A moment later, and he was looking out upon an altered world. There was no tram-lines, no pavement, no houses opposite. He saw coarse, greyish grasses stirring in a wind which cried out in an unfamiliar voice. Trembling violently, he unlocked the door and looked out.

A slim crescent of moon and a few stars dimly illumined a landscape without houses, a place grown suddenly strange and dreadful. Where the opposite villas should have been was the edge of a forest, thick and black and menacing. He stepped out, and his foot slid through spongy grass, ankle-deep in mud and slime. He looked back fearfully, and there was his shop with its open door, standing alone. The other jerry-built shops which linked up with it had vanished. It seemed forlorn and ridiculous and out of place, a toy shop standing alone in a wilderness.

Something cold fell on to his hand and made him start. Instantly he knew that it was a drop of sweat. His hair was saturated, his face running. Then he told himself that this was nightmare, that if he could but cry out aloud he would wake up. He cried out and heard his voice ring out hoarsely over the surrounding desolation. From the forest, the cry' of some wild animal answered him.

No, this was no dream, or, if it were, it was one of a kind altogether beyond his experience. Where was he? And how had he come to step out of his door into some strange place thousands of miles away from Nesthall?

But was he thousands of miles or—thousands of years? An unwontedly quick perception made him ask the question of himself. The land around him was flat, after the dreary nature of Middlesex. Fronting him, a few miles away, was the one hill which he had seen every day of his life, so that he knew by heart the outline of it against the sky. But it was Harrow Hill no more. A dense forest climbed its slope. And over all there brooded an aching silence charged with terror.

Curiosity had in him, to some extent, the better of fear. Cautiously he moved a little away from his shop, but cast continual backward glances at it to make sure that it was still there, while he stepped lightly and carefully over the swampy ground. Away to the left were open marshlands, and he could see a wide arc of the horizon. He could see no river, but vaguely he made out the contours of what he knew to be the Thames Valley. And not a house nor any living thing in sight!

He turned once more to look at his shop. It was still there, its open door spilling light on the bog grasses which grew to the edge of the threshold. And as he turned he saw a low hill away to his half-left—a hill which he could not recognize. He had taken a dozen steps towards it when his heart missed a beat, and he heard himself scream out aloud in an agony of terror.

The hill moved!

It was not a slow movement. There was something impetuous and savage in this sudden heaving-up of the huge mound. With movement the mass took shape from shapelessness. He saw outlined against the dim sky a pair of blunt ears set on a flat, brainless, reptilian head. Shapeless webbed feet tore at the ground in the ungainly lifting of the huge and beastly carcase. Two dull red lights suddenly burned at Trimmer, and he realized that the monster was staring at him.

As it stared he saw the long slit of a mouth open, and a great tongue, a dirty white in colour, passed in slobbery expectation over the greenish lips.

There was that about the movement which caused the soul of Trimmer to grow sick within him.

New terror broke the spell cast by the old. The nerves of motion were given back to him. He turned and ran, screaming wildly, arms outflung, towards the open door of his shop.

Behind him he heard the Thing lumbering in clumsy pursuit. The ground reverberated suddenly under its huge webbed feet. He heard the long reptilian body flopping heavily in his wake, heard its open mouth emitting strange wheezing cries full of a hateful yearning.

It was moving quickly, too. The sounds behind him gained upon him with a maddening rapidity. He could smell the creature's hot foetid breath. With one last despairing effort he gained the door of his shop and flung himself across the threshold into what seemed but a paltry chance of safety. Frenziedly he kicked out behind him at the door, closing it with a crash, and fell gasping across his counter.

Almost on the instant the little clock on the shelf began to strike. And sharp upon the stroke he heard a sudden moaning outside. His strained heart leaped again, but in the fraction of a moment he had recognized the sound. It was the tram resuming what had seemed to him its interrupted journey. The clock went on striking. He looked at it in blank bewilderment. It was striking the hour of twelve, midnight.

Now he had paid little attention to time, but estimated that he had spent something like half an hour in the strange and awful world outside his shop. Yet it had turned a minute to twelve when the change happened. And now here was his clock only just striking the hour.

He staggered to the door, and as he did so the tram passed, throwing a procession of twinkling lights along the top of his window. The curtain on the door was still raised a little, showing where he had peeped out. He looked through and saw gleaming tram-rails, the familiar pillar-box on the comer, the garden gate of Holmecroft opposite. Wherever he had been he was—and he thanked God for it—back in Today.

The clock finished striking the hour, the sounds of the tram grew fainter in the distance, and silence recaptured her hold upon the night. Trimmer edged away from the door. He was still sweating profusely, and his heart was still racing. He looked down at his feet. His cheap, worn boots were quite dry.

'God!' he ejaculated aloud. 'What a dream!'

A fit of shuddering seized him

'That thing! Ugh! It was like one of them things on the postcards what chase the pre'istoric blokes—only worse! I didn't dream that! I couldn't have done! I couldn't have run like that and yelled like I did, in a dream. I couldn't have been so surprised, and reasoned things out so clear! Besides, 'ow could I have fallen asleep like that in one second? No, it wasn't no dream! Then what—what in God's name was it?'

III

Next day Trimmer's few regular customers noticed that he looked ill and preoccupied. He handed the wrong article and the wrong change. His lips moved as if he were talking to himself.

As a matter of fact, he was trying to convince himself that his experience of the night before was a dream—trying and failing. What he half believed was something at which his Cockney common-sense rose in rebellion. By some law contrary to that of Nature he had been free to wander in another age while Time, as we count it, had stood still and waited for him. Either that or he was mad.

He determined to keep his clock exactly right according to Greenwich time, and be on the watch that night just before the stroke of twelve to see if the same thing happened again. But this time he would not venture out of today, would not leave his shop and risk the nameless dangers that awaited him in another age.

Eagerly and yet fearfully he awaited the coming of night. At nine o'clock he went down to the Station Hotel and stayed there until closing time, drinking brandy. Having returned to his shop, he paced the parlour at the back until ten minutes to twelve, when he took a candle into the shop and waited. Fearfully he stared through the lifted blind on the door and out over the steam-tarred road. It was raining gently, and he saw the drops dancing on the surface of a puddle. He watched them until he had almost hypnotised himself; until -

He felt himself start violently. It was as if the road and the house opposite had given themselves a sudden, convulsive twitch. Suddenly and amazingly it was not dark, but twilight. Opposite him, instead of a row of houses, was a hedge, with a rude rustic gate set in it. He found himself looking across fields. He saw a cluster of cows, a haystack, beyond a further hedge the upturned shafts of a derelict plough.

The road was still there, but it had changed out of knowledge. It was narrower, rutted, and edged with grass. As he looked he heard a jingling of bells, and a phaeton, with big yellow wheels, drawn by a high-stepping white horse, came gliding past.

Wonder rather than fear was his predominating emotion. The musical tooting of a horn startled him, and he heard the crisp sound of trotting horses and the lumbering of heavy wheels.

Into view came a coach and four, with passengers inside and out, a driver, with many capes, and a guard perched up behind pointing his long, slim horn at Harrow Hill. Immediately he recognized their clothes as something like those he had seen in pictures, on the covers of the boys' highwaymen stories he read and sold.

'It's safe enough,' he reflected, with a strange elation. 'Why, it ain't more than a hundred and fifty years ago!'

He wrenched open the door of his shop and passed out into the twilight of a June evening in the eighteenth century. Looking back, he saw that his shop stood alone as before, but this time it broke the line of a hawthorn hedge, on which red and white blossom was decaying and dying. The scent of it blended in his nostrils with the odour of new-mown hay.

He felt now eager and confident, entirely fearless. He was safe from the prehistoric horror that had attacked him the night before. Why, he was in an age of beer and constables and cricket matches.

With light steps he began to walk up the road towards London. It was his privilege now to wander without danger in another age, and see things which no other living man had ever seen. An old yokel, leaning against a gate, stared at him, went on staring, and, as he drew nearer, climbed the gate and made his way hurriedly across a hayfield. This reminded him that he looked as strange to the people of this age as they looked to him. He wished he had known, so that he could have hired an old costume and thus walked inconspicuously among them.

He must have walked half a mile without coming upon one single familiar landmark. A finger-post told him what he already knew—that he was four miles from Ealing Village. He paused outside an inn to read a notice which announced that the stage-coach Highflyer, plying between London and Oxford would arrive at the George at Ealing (D.V.) at 10.45 a.m. on Mondays, Wednesdays and Fridays. He was turning away, having read the bill, when he first saw Miss Marjory.

She was, if you please, a full seventeen years of age, and husband-high according to the custom of her times. She wore a prim little bonnet, a costume of royal blue, and carried a silk parasol which, when open, must have looked ludicrously small. He had one full glance at her piquantly pretty face and saw, for the fraction of an instant, great blue eyes staring at him in frank wonderment. She lowered her gaze abruptly, with an air of conscious modesty, when she saw that he had observed her.

Hitherto, as far as the strange circumstances permitted, Trimmer had felt entirely normal. That is to say that his emotions and outlook were in keeping with a man of his age, station, education and habit of mind. Now came a change, sudden, bewildering, well-nigh overwhelming.

Once he had been in a state which, for want of a better phrase, he called being 'in love'. He had 'walked out' with a young lady who was a draper's assistant. After a while she had deserted him because of the superior attractions of a young clerk in a warehouse. He had been wounded, but not deeply wounded. Marriage was not necessary to his temperament, or, as he put it, he could get along without women. Not for the last sixteen years had he thought of love until that moment, when he, the waif of another century, beheld Miss Marjory.

It was as if some strange secret were revealed to him on the instant. The ecstasy of love which engulfed him like a wave told him that here was his true mate, his complement according to Nature, born into this world, alas! One hundred and fifty years too early for him. Yet, for all that, by a miracle of witchcraft, by some oversetting of the normal laws, the gulf had been bridged, and they stood now face to face. He walked towards her, fumbling in his mind for something to say, some gallantry preliminary to street flirtations such as happened around him every day.

'Good evening, miss,' he said.

He saw the blush in her cheek deepen, and she answered without regarding him, 'Oh, sir, I pray you not to molest me. I am an honest maiden alone and unprotected.'

'I'm not molestin' you, miss. And you needn't be alone and unprotected unless you like.'

The maiden's eyelids flickered up and then down again.

'Oh, fie on you, sir!' she said. 'Fie on you for a bold man! I would have you know that my father is a highly respected mercer and drives into London daily in his own chaise. I have been brought up to learn all the polite accomplishments. 'T' would not be seemly for me to walk and talk with strangers.'

'There's exceptions to every rule, miss.'

Once more she gave him a quick modest glance.

'Nay, sir, but you have a pretty wit. 'Tis said that curiosity is a permitted weakness to us women. I vow that you are a foreigner. Your accents and strange attire betray you. Yet I have not the wit to guess whence you come, nor the boldness to ask.'

'I am as English as you are, Miss,' Trimmer protested, a little hurt.

The ready blush came once more to her cheek.

'Your pardon, sir, if I did mistake you for one of those mincing Frenchies. Nay, be not offended. I have heard tell that there is something vastly attractive about a Frenchy, so, if I made the error, I - Oh, why does my tongue betray my modesty!'

'I don't know, miss. But what about a little walk?'

She broke into a delightful little laugh.

'Sir, you speak a strange tongue and wear strange clothes. Yet I confess I find both to my mind. Doubtless you wonder how it is that you find a young lady like myself promenading alone at fall of evening. Ah, me, I fear that Satan is enthroned in my heart! I am acting thus to punish my papa.'

Trimmer made an incoherent noise.

'He promised to take me to Bath, and broke his promise,' she continued.
'Oh, sir, what crimes are done to the young in the name of Business! He has not the time, if I would credit such a tale! So, to serve him, he shall hear that his daughter walked abroad at

evening unattended, like any common Poll or Moll. You may walk with me a few yards if it be your pleasure, sir—but only a few yards. I would not have my papa too angry with his Marjory.'

From then he had no count of time. He walked with her in a sort of dream-ecstasy, while veil after veil of darkness fell over the fields of pasture and half-grown com. When at last she insisted that the time had come for parting he stole a kiss from her, a theft at which she more than half connived. In a low voice she confessed to him that she was not so sure of her heart as she had been at sunset.

Trimmer walked back on air to where his shop stood, alone and incongruous. He had learned the true meaning of love, and was drunk with an emotion which hitherto he had scarcely sipped. They had made an assignation for the following evening; for he believed that he had been fated to meet her, and that his shop door would let him out once more into the eighteenth century.

When he returned to his shop he was aware of one strange thing—that while it was visible to him it was invisible to others in the world to which it gave him access. He expected to find a crowd around it on his return, so queer and incongruous must it have looked to eighteenth century eyes. But only a rustic couple was strolling in the moonlight, on the other side of the road, and as he crossed the threshold it must have seemed to them that he had vanished into thin air, for he heard a shrill scream, which ceased on the instant as the clock struck the first beat of twelve.

He was back once more in the twentieth century, his heart full of a girl who was a hundred and fifty years away. He was like a boy after his first kiss under a moonlit hedge. Tomorrow night, he promised himself, if he could get back to the eighteenth century, he would remain in it, marry Marjory and live out his life, secure in the knowledge that Time was standing still and awaiting his return.

IV

Next morning the change in Charles Trimmer was still more marked. There was a far-off look in his eyes and a strange smile on his lips.

'If I didn't know ole Charlie,' said Mr Bunce, the butcher, to a friend, over the midday glass, 'I should think he was in love.'

Trimmer cared little about what his neighbours thought of him, nor had he any longer a regard for his business. His whole mind was centred upon the coming of midnight when, perhaps, he could step out across the years and take Marjory into his arms. He had not thought for anything else. Not having heard of La Belle Dame Sans Merci he saw no danger in his obsession. If he had it would have been the same.

Strangely enough he did not trouble himself greatly as to how he had come by this strange gift. He gave little thought to the old cross-eyed woman who had bestowed it upon him, nor did he speculate much as to what strange powers she possessed. Enough that the gift was his.

It was a world of dazzling white which Trimmer saw when he peeped through the blind that night. It startled him a little, for he had not thought of seeing snow. There was no saying now what period he would step into outside his shop. Snow was like a mask on the face of Nature.

For a thinking space he was doubtful if he should venture out, but the fear of missing Marjory compelled him. His teeth chattered as he plunged knee-deep into a drift, but he scrambled up over a small mound, on which the snow was only ankle-deep, and beneath him the surface was hard, possibly that of a road. He turned his face towards London, wondering whether the snow concealed the friendly pastures of the eighteenth century or the wilderness of some unguessed-at period of time.

Away to his left, looking in a straight line midway between Harrow Hill and London, he could see a forest holding aloft a canopy of snow'. He had forgotten if he had seen a wood in that direction on the occasion when he had met Marjory. He tried to rack his brains as he trudged on, shivering, hands deep in his pockets.

He had walked perhaps half a mile on what certainly seemed some sort of a track, without passing a house or any living person, when a sound, which he associated with civilization, smote upon his ears. It was the low, mournful howling of a dog.

The howling was taken up by other dogs, he could not guess how many, but the effect of it was weird and infinitely mournful. As nearly as he was able to locate them, the sounds came from the direction of the forest. Vaguely he wondered whose dogs they were and why they were howling. Perhaps they were cold, poor devils. People in less advanced times were very likely cruel to their dogs. They left them out, even on such nights as this.

He trudged on, listening to this intermittent howling and baying, which became more frequent and sounded nearer. Vague fears began to assail him.

He was not afraid of dogs which had been made domestic pets—the Fidos and Rovers and Peters of the happy twentieth century. But suppose these were savage—wild?

He halted doubtfully, and as he halted he saw some of them for the first time. There were six of them, and they were streaming across the snowfield from the direction of the forest, one slightly in advance of the others. They were barking and squealing, like hounds hot upon a scent. Their leader, a lean grey brute, raised his head, and uttered a loud yelp, and as he did so Trimmer saw that his eyes were luminous and burning, like two red coals.

In response to the creature's yelp the whole fringe of the wood became alive with his kind. The darkness was specked with vicious luminous eyes. Over the snowfield came the pack, as a black cloud crosses the sky. Trimmer uttered a little sharp cry of fear.

'Wolves!' he gasped aloud. 'Wolves!'

As he turned and ran an echo of an old history lesson came back to his mind. He remembered having been told that hundreds and hundreds of years ago the English forests were haunted by wolves, which, maddened by hunger in the winter-time, would attack and kill whomsoever ventured abroad. He ran like a blind man, stumbling and slipping, with horror and despair storming at his heart.

In the distance he could see his shop, with the safe warm light gleaming like a beacon, but he knew that he could never reach it. The yelping of his pursuers grew nearer every moment. Already he could hear their scampering in the snow behind him. A minute later, and a lean body shot past his thigh, just missing him. He heard the snap of the brute's jaws as it rolled over in the snow. Then sharp teeth gripped and tore the calf of one of his legs, and he heard amid his terror a worrying snarl as he tried to kick himself free.

More teeth gripped his shoulder. There was a weight on his back—more weight—and terror which drugged physical pain. One arm was seized above the elbow. They were all over him now, snapping, snarling, tearing and worrying. Down they dragged him—down into the snow—down. . . .

The policeman, passing the shop of Charles Trimmer at nine in the morning, was surprised to find it not yet open. The daily papers had been left in a pile on the doorstep by the van-boy who had evidently despaired of making anyone hear. Being suspicious, the constable examined the door and found that the green blind was lifted a little. Through the chink he could see an eye peering out; but it was an eye which seemed not to see.

Having called out several times and rapped on the glass without evoking any reply, the policeman broke in at the back. He found Charles Trimmer kneeling by the shop door, peering out under the green blind. He was quite dead.

There was not a mark on him, but a doctor giving evidence before the coroner explained that his heart was in a bad way—it weighed a great deal more than a man's heart ought to weigh—and he had been liable for some time to die suddenly. A nightmare or any sudden shock might have brought this about at any time.

The verdict was in accordance with the evidence.

The Wrong Station

We had been together in the miserable waiting-room at Ixtable Junction nearly a quarter of an hour, and had not spoken for no better reason, perhaps, than that we were Englishmen. The fire was nearly out, and the light of the gas lamp showed signs of following its bad example. A dense fog had thrown the train service into utter confusion. It was not at all a cheerful kind of night.

My companion was a man of fifty, of medium height, rather grey, and certainly not handsome. He was dressed comfortably but not well. His long black overcoat and bowler hat, neither of which was shabby, seemed to make him appear more commonplace than he need have looked. He had big, fishy-looking eyes, and a large, untidy moustache with a pathetic droop to its ends. He had with him a heavy valise. He looked what I afterwards found him to be—a commercial traveller of the not too prosperous kind.

For a long while he sat fidgeting, staring down at his bag, which rested beside him on the floor. Then suddenly he sprang up and crossed the room to examine a map of the line hanging on the opposite wall. He frowned over it for a full minute, his eyes following a moving thumbnail. Then he turned to me.

'It was somewhere between Reading and Plymouth,' he said.

'I beg your pardon?'

'It was somewhere between Reading and Plymouth. Do you know that part well, sir?'

'Pretty well. Why?'

His big, fishy eyes were fixed on me in a stare of pathetic appeal.

'If I could only remember the name of that station! If I saw it anywhere, if somebody said it, I should know it at once. A beautiful name it is. It's always just on the edge of my memory, but I can never quite get it.'

'That's rather awkward,' I said, 'if you want to go there.'

'I do, sir, I do! I was a fool ever to leave. I ought to have stood up for myself and refused to go. But she persuaded me. And now I don't suppose I shall ever find that little town again.'

'If there's a station there,' I said, puzzled and amused, 'it must be on the map. But perhaps it's on the Southern Railway.'

'No, the Great Western it was—a train that gets you into Plymouth in about four and a half hours, and lands you there in the small hours of the morning I know most of the towns along that route, too—Newbury, Westbury, Taunton, Exeter, but it wasn't any of them. I wonder if you know the place I want?' He laughed a little shamefacedly. 'Everybody thinks I'm mad when I tell them. '

'It all sounds very mysterious,' I said. 'I gather that you've been to some place that took your fancy very much, and that you want to go there again, only you don't happen to remember the name of it?'

'That's it,' he said, eagerly. 'I tell you I'd know that name at once directly I saw it or heard it. But it's not on any map. Every time I see a map I go and have a look. It happened about two years ago, and I've been worrying about it all this time.'

My curiosity was by then sufficiently aroused to make me want to hear the whole story. There was nothing of the madman or the romancer about this commonplace little man with his big bag and his air of petty commerce.

'What was your town like?' I asked.

He turned his eyes away from me and seemed to think.

'Well—I only saw a bit of it, but I'd like to have seen all. There's not such another place in England—in the whole world, for that matter. I don't mean only because it was pretty, but there was something in the air—I can't very well explain. If you like, I'll tell you just how everything happened. Perhaps you'll laugh. Most people do.'

I promised not to.

'Oh, I don't mind. Nineteen people in twenty say there's no such place, tell me I dreamt it all, but I know I didn't. I do have dreams, of course, but they're never clear like that, and anybody knows the difference between a dream and a fact. '

'I always do,' said I, to give him confidence.

'Of course, of course!' He sat down on the yellow bench under the map he had been studying, and looked away from me into the grey embers of the dying fire. 'There's one or two things I ought to explain first of all,' he said. 'I'm not a bit an imaginative sort of man, and I'm not what you'd call poetical. I've been in business ever since I was thirteen, and if I didn't begin with a pretty hard head, I've got one now, I give you my word. Very well! Another thing is I'm a married man with four kids. We've got a nice little home at Willesden. I'm a good father and a good husband, though I say it who shouldn't. The missus and me have been married eighteen years, and we're still pretty fond of each other. Not quite like we were at first, mind you, but only fools 'ud expect that. Still, I'd cut off my hand for her if need be. You take me, sir?'

'Perfectly.'

'Well, I travel for a big firm of comb manufacturers, and at that time, two years ago, I was taken off my usual round to work up what we call the Western circuit. That's the whole country of Cornwall and about half Devonshire, beginning with Plymouth. The man on there had been making rather a mess of things—young man without much go and less experience. So they put me on there to buck things up a bit.

'I caught the night express from Paddington, and had the good luck to get a compartment to myself. Plymouth was the first stop, and I tipped the guard to wake me up there if I went to sleep, for I didn't want to find myself at Penzance or Falmouth next morning.

'I read for the best part of an hour, and then began to feel sleepy. We whizzed through a big station, and I looked out and saw that it was Reading. I leaned back and put my feet on the opposite seat. I didn't feel very well. I had a sort of feeling—I can't describe it—that I generally get before a heart attack. I've got a bad heart. It may last me for years yet, or it may carry me off tonight. You can't really tell with these things. I've got to be careful of myself.

'Well, that night I was sure it was going to give me a doing, within an hour or two. However, I'd got some stuff the doctor gave me, and I took the bottle out of my breast-pocket and had a pull at it. Then I dropped off to sleep, which rather surprised me afterwards, for generally I keep awake when I'm feeling queer. And when I woke up I felt better than I'd ever felt before.'

He paused and looked at me. His great ugly eyes were shining with a light that made them almost beautiful.

'I don't mean only better in health. I felt as I used to feel when I was a nipper—a kind of lightness—I'd never felt it since. I swear I could have danced without music, or run, or jumped—that kind of feeling. The train had stopped. "Halloa!" I thought, "this is Plymouth. That guard ought to have called me."

'Just as those words were going through my mind the door opened and a railway man put his head into the compartment. He wasn't my guard, but some other, or, perhaps, a porter—I didn't look to see what he was. But he was extraordinary to look at— extraordinary! I've never used the word before when speaking of a man, but he was beautiful. Yes, sir, there's not another word in the language to describe his looks. I'd never seen a man's face like his before. There's one or two pictures of angels in the National Gallery a bit like him, but that's the nearest I've come to seeing his like. And what does he do, but call me by my Christian name.

' "This is your station, Harry," he said, as gravely as you please.

'I wasn't a bit offended, only a little surprised.

' "What, Plymouth?" says I.

' "No, not Plymouth."

'I looked out, and there was the name of the station on a board, the lovely name I can't remember. And when I saw it I knew that I must get out. It didn't matter if I missed all my appointments the next day. I had to get out there. And yet—and yet, somehow I didn't want to.

'The porter took hold of me by the arm. "Come on, Harry," he said. "It's a beautiful town, the most beautiful town in all the world."

' "But I've got to go on to Plymouth," I said, making a kind of struggle.

"I'll come here later on; I will, really. I don't want to get out here now. Let me go on to Plymouth."

'The man put his mouth close to my ear. His voice was very soft and wheedling, just like a woman's.

' "It's such a lovely town, Harry," he whispered. "Don't be afraid"

'Well, I let him lead me out on to the platform, and then I turned round for my bag. "We don't take luggage here," he said, and it seemed to me at the time perfectly reasonable. I know this sounds like a dream to you, but it was real—real!

'The porter left me. I don't know if he got on to the train or not, but presently I was all alone on the platform. I lingered for a moment, and then started out to see the town.

'It must have been somewhere round two in the morning, and quite dark. But it wasn't an ordinary darkness, it was a kind of deep blue. And there was a smell of flowers in the air, faint but very refreshing. I don't know where it came from, for I saw no gardens. I walked down a kind of alley, just as you find at the entrance of any ordinary station, into one of the streets of that town.'

He fixed me with his great eyes, held his speech for a moment, and then burst out, 'Oh, my God! That wonderful town!'

He relapsed into silence, as if a little ashamed of his emotion. After a pause he went on, 'It doesn't sound so much to describe—not the place itself. The street was wide, and on each side was a row of large old houses, with diamond panes to the windows, and tops storeys projecting out over the ground floors. There were lights in several of the windows, and they reflected on the pavements so that the diamond panes looked like lattice work of light and shadow. And in most of the houses there was music and singing—wonderful music.

'I said the road was very wide. At one side a stream, lined with poplars, ran between two stone embankments. And little bridges of old red brick spanned the stream every few yards, one bridge to the front door of every house on that side. And the stream tinkled as it ran, for all the world as if somebody was playing the harp. Oh, I can't make you feel what it was like—the old houses, the stream, the bridges, the blue darkness, the scents, the music.

'I saw nobody about but children. Yes, there were children playing in the road at that hour of the morning! They played hide-and-seek behind the bridges and danced and laughed and sang. Such children, believe me! I never cared much for kids, except my own, but I didn't mind them playing around me, and instead of growling at those who caught hold of the skirt of my coat, I turned and patted their heads, and laughed because they were laughing.

'I had not gone far when I came to a house I seemed to know. At least, if I didn't know it, I seemed to know that I ought to go there—that I was expected. I didn't stop to ask questions of myself; I just went up to the door and knocked. And presently a young girl opened it to me.'

He stopped again.

'That is the queerest thing of all. This is where everybody laughs, and you'll laugh too. I was an ugly old devil then, just the same as I am now. No girl had looked at me twice in the last twenty years. I'd got my wife, I'd settled down; it was a long time since I'd thought of girls. But at the sight of her my heart beat like a boy's, and I knew that I knew her, that we had loved each other for God knows how many years.

'And I remembered her just as I should remember the name of that town if somebody told it to me, only it was a long memory. It seemed to go back hundreds and hundreds of years. And I loved her with a kind of love I had never felt before—and I knew that she loved me. At the sight of her, something in me changed. I wasn't any longer an ugly, common little man, beginning to grow old. I was young again, and as fine a gentleman as any in the land. I could feel it in my very blood.

'She uttered a little cry, and called me by a name that I knew had once belonged to me, only I'd forgotten it. I've forgotten it again since. I can only remember her look and the tone of her voice. She ran right into my arms and kissed me, and laughed and cried over me, and my brain reeled and reeled with happiness, for I had been waiting for such a long while for that moment to come.

'My wife seemed a long way away, and it didn't seem as if I was being the least unfaithful to her. It seemed as if, in marrying her, I'd done this girl who was clinging to me some little wrong. She had been first, she had come hundreds and hundreds of years before the other woman who lay asleep in our little house at Willesden

' "Let me come in," I remember saying to the girl who clung to me, and when I said that she began to cry. It was all a mistake, she said, and I would have to go back to the station and catch the next train. I mustn't stop; and she had been waiting for me for so long! We must both wait a little longer, and it was such a pity, because now I had had a peep at that town, and seen her, and I shouldn't be happy or contented any more until I came back.

'I said I wasn't going back to catch the next train or any other train, but she said I must. She said the time had not yet come and that somebody had made a mistake. She said that the porter ought to have let me go on to Plymouth—and somehow the word Plymouth sounded queer coming from her.

'I stood there, suddenly very miserable. I didn't want to go. I wanted to stay with her and live in that old house beside the stream, and play with the children, and go on feeling young. And I began to beg of her to let me stop.

'But she wouldn't hear me. She said they'd called me out at the wrong station, and that I must go on to Plymouth, but one day I would come back. And somehow I couldn't argue with her much. I seemed to have no will.

'I wish I'd stood up for myself now. I'd found my way there and it didn't seem fair to send me away. But she took me by the hand, and together in silence we went back the way I had come through the bluish night. And those wonderful children played around us as we walked.

'There was a train waiting at the station, and we stood on the platform for a moment and kissed goodbye. She said I must be patient and I would soon come back. She had been patient, too, and she had been waiting for me so long, she whispered. So I got into the train and it started off, and then—then I tried to remember the name of that station, and couldn't.

'After a while I dropped asleep, and when I woke up there was a doctor and two railway men in the compartment, and they were pouring brandy down my throat, and seemed rather surprised to find I was alive. We were at Plymouth now, and it seemed I'd nearly died in my sleep, and only the brandy had pulled me through.

'The doctor said he quite thought I was dead when they fetched him to look at me, and I must say I've never had quite such a bad turn as that before or since. I never travel without something in my pocket now, in case of accidents.'

He paused and in the ensuing silence we heard the sound of an approaching train.

'Mine,' he said. 'I'm going on to Charr. Well, that's the story, and whatever you say won't convince me that it was a dream. What do you make of it?'

But I could not tell him what I made of it.

The Room Over the Kitchen

I was dog-tired and bone-weary when my gaze welcomed from the knap of a hill the first lights of Penhiddoc. I had tramped farther than I had intended, and my rucksack, which had been a feather's weight at starting, had long since become an aching burden. The salt taste of the wind was enough to tell me that I had at last reached the coast. It was a sea wind, which blew with increasing violence at every gust, and although the rest of my way lay downhill I found it as hard as ever to put one foot before the other.

It was eight o'clock on a March evening, and I had been walking all day.

I had, I suppose, my share of that vanity which makes a man over-estimate his powers of endurance. A walking tour should be a pleasure, and I began to realize that I was a fool for allowing the last seven miles to be a penance.

As I tramped downhill through that raging wind, I hoped with all my heart that the first house would be an inn, and in that luck was with me. Two small windows spread ruddy light upon the road through drawn red blinds. Above them I could make out the dim outline of a signboard. I reached the door, and began groping for the latch. I had found it and lifted it, when I was aware of a movement behind me, and another hand came to rest upon my own.

It was a man's hand, but very long and thin and delicate. The fingers were cold, and although their grasp was firm and restraining, there was a quality of gentleness in their touch which at once banished alarm and even annoyance.

I turned as quickly as my weariness would let me, and found myself face to face with a slim young man, some inches taller than myself, who backed a step or two as I turned.

'What's the matter?' I said.

He seemed to speak with difficulty when he answered. His voice was cultured, but it was very thin and weak, and he spoke as if he needed a fresh breath for every word.

'If you are going to stay there,' he said, 'don't let them give you the room over the kitchen.'

The words were themselves sufficient to make me stare at him. He backed another step as I stared. The night behind him was as black as a sheet of carbon, and in the darkness he was all dim and shadowy.

'What do you mean?' I asked.

The wind seemed to carry his words past me. What I heard sounded like an echo.

'Don't let them give you the room over the kitchen.'

I was too tired to bandy words with this young man with the white, drawn face, who was probably a harmless lunatic.

'Oh, all right. Thank you,' I said, and opened the door.

Next moment I had shut him and the wind out in the night behind me, and found myself standing in a stone passage with the bar on my right hand.

In the bar a lighted oil-lamp hung from the ceiling, and a good log fire was burning on an open hearth.

Save for myself the bar was quite empty, and when I had slipped off my rucksack I rapped with my knuckles on a table before sitting down on the comer of a settle close to the fire. After half a minute an old man came shuffling in, and wished me good evening.

'Get me a pint of beer,' I said, 'and some bread and cheese. And can you put me up for the night?'

He thought for a moment.

'I'll have to speak to the missus about that, sir,' he said. 'I think we can manage 'ee. Been walking far? I expect you're tired. I'll go and see to the wittles first.'

While I ate and drank, my thoughts kept returning to the young man outside who had seized my hand as soon as it touched the latch. Why shouldn't I have the room over the kitchen? It reminded me of some incident in one of those old stories about strangers being robbed and murdered in lonely inns. There was something vaguely disquieting, even uncanny, about the happening. To regain some degree of mental comfort I had to remind myself that I was living in the twentieth century, and that mine host was too old and frail to be in any way formidable. But, perhaps because I was very tired and had used a great deal of my nervous energy, the incident lingered unpleasantly in my mind. I could still feel the touch of those fingers and hear that slow, thin, laboured voice.

The landlord came back while I was still eating, bringing his wife along with him. She was a few years younger, and seemed more energetic. She could give me a room for the night, she said, and some hot supper in about an hour, and would do her best to make me comfortable.

The old man threw more logs on the fire, and as a sudden gust of wind howled in the chimney he looked up at his wife and said, "Tes rough weather. 'Tes the sort o' night for Mr Farney to be about.'

I saw the woman frown at him, and asked quickly, 'Who is Mr Farney?'

I thought they exchanged quick glances, and the woman said, "Tes a saying in these parts when the wind's rough, sir. Shall I show 'ee the room now, sir, or will 'ee rest a bit longer?'

I was in no hurry to move, and said so. I edged closer to the fire, and filled and lit a pipe. Presently two or three working men came in, and the atmosphere of the room seemed to grow warmer and more cheerful. It was not until the smell of cooking warned me of the imminence of supper that I told the landlady I was ready to unpack my rucksack and have a wash.

Candle in hand, she led the way up a narrow flight of uncarpeted stairs, and ushered me into a bare low-ceilinged room which smelt cold and damp.

It looked clean, however, and it was at least as comfortable as I had any right to expect.

She set the candle down upon the chest of drawers, and was on her way to the door when I addressed her.

'Is the kitchen underneath here?' I asked.

She shot me a quick glance, half frightened, half questioning.

'Yes, sir,' she said, and after a pause she added, 'Why?'

'Oh, nothing,' I said. 'I only wanted to know.'

I am ashamed to say that I was as nervous as a child while I undid my rucksack and washed in the icy water from the ewer. I was ashamed of myself at the time, but there was no cure in asking myself what danger I had to fear. I hurried over my unelaborate toilet, and then set out, candle in hand, for the stairs.

The wind was still storming the draughty old house, and the passage outside my door was crossed and criss-crossed by sharp currents of air. Before I had time to shield the flame of my candle I was left in sudden darkness to blunder to the stairs as best I might.

Once I was on the stairs there was enough light to see what I was doing.

Light came through the open door of the bar, spreading a yellow flag on the stone passage below. I had hardly descended two steps when I became suddenly aware that there was somebody below me on the stairs. In another moment I had recognized the tall, thin young man who had addressed me so strangely outside the inn.

'Don't let them give you the room over the kitchen,' he said, in the same thin, laboured voice.

Having uttered his peculiar warning, he turned about, and I saw his long, slim figure cross the passage and enter the bar.

I hurried after him, set down the blown-out candle on the little counter, and turned to look at him. To my astonishment he was not there. Besides myself there were only three people in the bar—the landlord, his wife, and an old man in a fisherman's jersey.

A sensation of something like horror took hold of me. I stood staring at the three of them, and they stared back at me with round, bewildered eyes.

'What's the matter with my bedroom?' I said sternly to the landlord—'the room over the kitchen?'

'Nothing, sir. 'Tes the best room'

'Oh, I know all about that. But I've twice been warned not to sleep in it, and I want to know why. I want to know what it all means.'

There was a moment's dead silence, broken at last by the landlady's voice.

'Who warned 'ee, sir?'

'Oh, I don't know who it was. A tall, thin young man. He spoke to me outside, and just now on the stairs. Where is he?'

The woman turned at once to her husband.

'There!' she exclaimed. 'I knew it! I was sure as Mr Farney had spoken to 'un.'

'And who,' I asked, 'is Mr Farney? And, what is more, where is he?'

The landlord patted the bench beside him.

''Tes nothing to worry 'ee, sir,' he said. 'I swear there's naught the matter with the room. Come and sit 'ee down here, sir, and I'll tell 'ee about it. Take no notice o' Mr Farney. Poor souls like him, they don't know what they're sayin'. They've got but one thing on their minds, like, and they must out with it. They're like daft things. But sit 'ee down here, sir, and I'll tell 'ee.'

The old man's tone and manner reassured me, and I sat down.

'It must be nigh on twenty years ago,' he said, 'when four young gentlemen came in here one night. They was from Oxford, and walking like yourself—Mr Farney and his three friends. 'Twas a windy night like this, and just this time o' the year. They wanted to be put up, same as you.

'There was only two rooms for the four of 'em, but Mr Farney was a bit partikler like. He said as he couldn't sleep in the same room with anybody else, and nothing would do but he must have a room to 'eeself, and his three friends all in the other room. They was nice young gentlemen but fond of a lark, so while Mr Farney was unpacking they got 'old of Uncle William—he's dead now, poor dear—to tell a story about Mr Farney's room bein' haunted. Down comes Mr Farney, and Uncle William tells his story, and I tell a bit, too—God forgive me! And the others, they all laugh at Mr Farney, and tell him the room over the kitchen is haunted, and hadn't he better have one o' them to sleep along o' him? But Mr Farney said as he didn't mind ghosts—though 'twas plain he was nervous—and he must have a room to 'eeself, whether or no.

'Well, sir, you know how a joke sometimes gets worked up until it's beyond a joke. Maybe the three young gents all took too much to drink. Maybe we all did. And when Mr Farney had gone to bed, the others made up their minds to dress up in sheets and frighten 'un. And—they did!'

His voice quavered, and suddenly stopped.

'So, you see, sir, that's the reason, on windy nights like that one, Mr Farney stops strangers who're coming here and tells 'em not to have the room over the kitchen. But the room's right enough. 'Twas all a story Uncle William told 'un.'

I thought I was beginning to see.

'Good Lord!' I exclaimed. 'Do you mean to say the poor fellow went mad?'

'No, sir; don't you understand?' The old man laid a shaking hand on my arm. 'Mr Farney isn't real—not like you and me, sir. He died o' fear that night when the others frightened him—near twenty years ago!'

The Green Scarf

When the Wellingford family became extinct the days of Wellingford Hall as one of the great country homes of England were already numbered. The estate passed into the hands of commercial-minded people who had no reverence for the history of a great house. The acres around the old Hall became too valuable as building sites to be allowed to remain as a park surrounding a country mansion. So the fat Wellingford sheep were driven elsewhere to pasture, and surveyors and architects heralded the coming of navvies and builders.

All this happened many years ago. The old park became crossed and criss-crossed by new roads, and perky little villas with names like 'Ivyleigh' and 'Dulce Domum' sprang up like monstrous red fungi. Even these have since mellowed, and grown their own ivy and Virginia creeper, and put on airs of respectable maturity. The Hall itself, forlorn and abandoned, like some poor human wretch deserted in his old age, began slowly to crumble into decay.

Wellingford Hall was no more than an embarrassment to the new owners of the estate, who were willing to let it or sell it at the prospective tenant's or purchaser's own price; but to dispose of a great house with no land attached to it and surrounded by a garden city is no easy matter. It was too big for its environment. After some vicissitudes as a private school and the home of a small community of nuns, it was abandoned to its natural fate: 'for', said one of the directors of the Wellingford Estate Limited, a gentleman not above mixing his metaphors, 'what was the sense of keeping a white elephant in a state of repair?'

Three years before this present time of writing came Aubrey Vair, the painter, as poor as most other painters, a lover of old buildings and all the cobwebby branches of archaeology, and took Wellingford Hall at a weekly rental of fewer shillings than might be demanded for the use of a gardener's cottage. He knew one of the directors, and he had discovered that a few rooms in the middle of the block of buildings were still habitable. The directors, I suppose, wondered why anyone should wish to live in the damp-ridden, rat-riddled old hole, but they did not despise shillings, and they let him come.

Vair wrote me several letters, begging me to come down and rough it with him. It was just the place for a writer, he assured me; it would give me ideas. He had been searching after priests'-holes and had discovered no less than five. One of the great rooms made the finest studio he had yet painted in. And really, as regards comfort, he avowed, it wasn't so bad, so long as one came there already warned to expect only the amenities of a poor bachelor establishment. And then, he added temptingly, there were the historical associations.

I already knew something about the latter, having discovered my facts in a book dealing with old English country houses. Charles the First had spent a night there during the Great

Civil War. Charles the Second was supposed to have hidden there after the battle of Worcester. But best of all was the romantic tale of the capture and execution of Sir Peter Wellingford in 1649. Briefly, Sir Peter was a proscribed Royalist who lived hunted and in hiding after the failure of the royal arms. A wiser man would have crossed the Channel, but Sir Peter had a young wife at Wellingford Hall. He had often visited her in safety, and might have continued to do so, but for a traitor in his own household. This fellow, so the story went, betrayed his master by waving a green scarf from one of the windows, this being a pre-arranged signal to inform a detachment of Parliamentary troops that the head of the house was secretly in residence. The soldiers burst in at night, and ransacked the house before Sir Peter Wellingford, was discovered in a hiding-hole—or 'privacie', as the old chronicle described it. The cavalier was dragged outside and shot in his own courtyard.

Here was a story romantic enough to inveigle the fancy of most men with a grain of imagination. I fully intended to visit Wellingford Hall, but circumstances caused me to defer my intention for the first summer and it was not until the following May, when Vair had been in residence a full year, that I paid him my deferred visit. I journeyed by road, driving myself in my small two-seater, so that Vair had no opportunity to meet me, and I had my first view of Wellingford Hall before I could be biased by his enthusiasm.

Holy writ speaks of the abomination of desolation standing where it ought not; and here was this grim, forbidding, crumbling old ruin still surrounded by its moat and standing in the midst of jerry-built 'Chumleighs' and 'Rose-mounts'. It was like finding the House of Usher in the middle of a new garden city. In spite of its moat the Hall had never been intended for a fortress and the bridge I crossed must have been nearly as old as the house itself.

Vair heard me coming and pushed open the great nail-studded door under the archway of the main entrance to come out and greet me with a grin and a handshake. He climbed up beside me and directed me round into the yard, where there was plenty of accommodation for a dozen cars. Strangely enough, the stables and coach-houses were in better repair than the old house itself.

The hall had once been magnificent, but most of the ceiling was gone, and the oak balustrade of the staircase, having had a commercial value, had been long since removed. A trail of sacking across broken paving stones pointed the way to Vair's apartments beyond. He ushered me into a fine room, in quite a reasonable state of repair, furnished with products of his speculations at country auctions. Although the month was May the weather was none too warm, and I was glad of the sight of the log fire which lent the room an additional air of comfort. Vair laughed to hear me exclaim, and asked if I were ready for tea.

He lived there, he explained, entirely alone, except that a charwoman came each morning to do the rough work and cook his one hot meal of the day.

'You won't mind putting up with cold stuff and tinned things of an evening?' he asked anxiously.

I hate tinned foods, but, of course, I could not say so.

After tea, Vair showed me the rest of the rooms which he had made habitable, and, really, he had managed to make himself much more comfortable than I had expected. He had contrived—Heaven knows how—to learn a lot of intimate history of the old place, and blew the name by which every room had been called in the house's palmy days of dignity and prosperity. My bedroom, for instance, was known as 'Lady Ursula's Nursery', although history had long since forgotten who Lady Ursula was.

It was easy to see that Vair had a boyish enthusiasm for the place. He was a queer chap, with more than the average artist's share of eccentricities, and he believed in all manner of superstitions and pseudo sciences. He was one of those ageless men who might have been anything in the twenties, thirties, or forties. I happened to know that he was nearly fifty, but his thin wiriness of figure and boyish zest for life kept him youthful. Obviously his pleasure at having me down was not so much for my own sake as his. I was somebody to whom he could 'show off the house. He was clearly as proud of it as if it had been restored to its former dignity and he were the actual owner.

'For Heaven's sake, don't go about the place by yourself,' he said, 'or you'll break your neck. I've nearly broken mine a dozen times, and I'm beginning to know where it isn't safe to walk. It must be rather rare to find damp-rot and dry-rot in the same house, but we've got both here.'

I promised faithfully that I wouldn't move without him. Even the main staircase did not appear too safe to me, but Vair assured me that it was all right. After tea he took me over such parts of the house as it was safe to visit, but I shall make no attempt to describe most of this pilgrimage. My memory carries dreary pictures of damp and decay, of dust and dirt, and cobwebs, mouldering walls and crumbling floors. The old place must have been a warren of secret rooms and passages, and he showed me those he had discovered. All I can say is that the refugees of the bad old days must have been very uncomfortable, and those who escaped deserved to.

One large room under the roof, which we visited, had once been a secret chamber. It was called the Chapel, and here Mass had been said in defiance of the law throughout part of the sixteenth and seventeenth centuries.

'There must be a lot more secret rooms,' Vair remarked. 'Little Owen, who was a master at constructing such places, is known to have spent months here during the reign of Elizabeth. The house was always being raided, and the raiders had little satisfaction.'

'They got the poor old cavalier,' I laughed.

'Oh, yes. But he was given away, or sold, by a servant. I've shown you the place where I'm almost sure he hid—behind where the bed-head used to be in the room called the King's Chamber. We'll see if we can find some more while you're here, if you like.'

It suddenly occurred to me that Vair had always called himself 'sensitive' or psychic, and it was perhaps natural of me to put on the non-committal smile of the polite sceptic and inquire if he had seen any ghosts. Rather to my surprise, he shook his head.

'No,' he answered; 'it isn't at all that kind of place. The house is quite friendly. I should have felt it at once if it had been otherwise.'

'But I should have thought with its history'

'Ah, it's seen troubled days, but they were always nice people who lived here. There are no dreadful legends of bloodshed and cruelty. '

'There is the story of the cavalier,' I objected. 'Surely his ghost ought to haunt the place.'

'Why? He was a good man from all accounts and he died a man's death. Only troubled or wicked people linger about the scenes of their earth-life. When he was taken out and slaughtered all the hatred and blood-lust came from outside. If any impressions of those spent passions remain, they're not inside the house, and I don't want them inside.'

I smiled to myself, knowing that, from Vair's point of view, the house ought to be haunted, and his excuses for the non-appearance of a ghost or two struck me as ingenious but far-fetched.

'That's a pity,' I said, tongue in cheek. 'I quite hoped to be introduced to a Grey lady or a Spectre Cavalier.'

He frowned, knowing that I was laughing at him.

'Well, you won't be,' he said, 'unless '

'Unless what?'

'Well, unless something happens to alter present conditions. If, for instance, we were to find something which someone long forgotten desired should remain hidden.'

'I see.'

'I doubt if you do. And I doubt if anything could be done now to disturb any of the Wellingfords in their long sleep. They seem to have been an ideal family; I haven't been able to find a word of scandal on any page of their history. Where there has once been bitterness and hatred, there you may look for ghosts. There was none here. All that came from outside. That frenzied desire, for instance, to trap and kill a man because he had fought for his king, long after his cause was well lost; that bitter bigotry which sought to prevent folk from worshipping according to their consciences. It all came from outside, I tell you!'

Vair's voice had risen. Like most men with no particular faith he respected all creeds and religious intolerance always moved him to violent anger. Respect for his deadly seriousness kept my face grave.

'Do you mean just outside?' I asked.

'How do I know? And so long as they remain outside what does it matter? I assure you, I don't want them brought in.'

To my relief, he then veered away from a subject which was hardly within my scope of conversation. There was little of the mystic in me. All the same, when at last I retired to bed in Lady Ursula's nursery, I was glad to remember that Vair had given the house a clean bill of health in the psychic sense. By the time I had been Vair's guest for twenty-four hours I had begun to feel with him that the old ruin had a kindly and friendly atmosphere, in spite of its apparent gloom, and that this might have been the legacy of good people who had lived and died within its walls.

At the risk of giving this narrative an air of being disconnected, I must pass hurriedly over the next two or three days of my visit, for they brought forth little that is worth recording. Sometimes Vair did a little painting, and then his preoccupation drove me to my own work. We did a little fishing and sometimes walked three-quarters of a mile to the Wellingford Arms where, according to Vair, who accounted himself an expert, the bitter beer was better than the average. Sometimes we risked our necks on rickety stairs and crumbling floors, looking for more secret hiding-places, an occupation in which I soon became infected with some of Vair's schoolboy zest.

The place was quiet enough during the day, but the villas and bungalows which had marched almost to the edge of the moat made themselves audible at night. Every Lyndhurst and Balmoral seemed able to boast of a musical daughter or a powerful gramophone. The effect of sitting in one of those dignified old rooms with the windows open and hearing echoes from the musical comedies was grotesque in the extreme. Vair had evidently grown used to it, for he made no comment.

I had arrived on a Saturday, and it was on the afternoon of the Tuesday following that, between us, we made a discovery of historical interest; a discovery which we came afterwards bitterly to regret having made. We were on the first floor landing, where long windows, deep in a recess, looked out over the Wellingford Park estate, when Vair mentioned that he had never examined the window seats.

'Sliding panels,' he said, 'certainly have existed, but they belong mostly to fiction. They were too hard to construct and too easily discovered. Take the five hiding-places you've seen in this house. Three of them are behind fireplaces, one under the stairs, and the other must have been masked at one time by the head of a bedstead. Window-seats were very often used, and this one looks likely. Let's try it.'

We rapped it with our knuckles and, although it did not sound hollow, there was obviously an empty space beneath it. We pushed and tugged and teased the surface of the wood with our fingers. And suddenly I saw a crack widen, and part of the seat which had fitted into the rest of the woodwork as neatly as a drawer came away in my hands, and we stared at each other with laughter and curiosity in our eyes.

'Hallo, what's this!' Vair exclaimed.

The cavity disclosed was very small. It was obviously not the entrance to any place of concealment capable of holding a human being. I lit a match and thrust it down into the darkness. Then cheek by jowl we peered together into a cavity no more than three feet deep.

'Nothing here,' I said, breaking cobwebs as I moved my wrist to and fro.

'Isn't there!' exclaimed Vair.

He brushed me aside and his arm disappeared up to the shoulder. His hand was black when he drew it forth, and an end of something like a black rag was between his fingers. It was an old piece of silk, so rotten with age that it almost crumbled under our touch; but when we had blown on it and brushed it with our fingers we saw that it owed its present colour to the dirt of ages, and that it had once been green. On the instant the old tale leaped into the minds of both of us, and we exclaimed together, 'The Green Scarf!'

I forget what we said for the first minute or two. We were both excited and elated. There is some peculiar pleasure, difficult to analyse or explain, in discovering a relic which serves to corroborate some old tale or passage of ancient history. We neither of us doubted that we had discovered the green scarf by which Sir Peter Wellingford had been betrayed nearly three hundred years before.

'The traitor must have kept it here in readiness,' said Vair, his eyes dancing, 'and when he'd signalled he dropped it back again, and there it's lain from that day to this.'

'And most likely,' I added, taking the relic from his hands, 'this is the very' window he waved from.'

The window was open and I leaned out and let the dingy rag flutter from my hand in the warm afternoon breeze.

'Don't!' said Vair sharply, and pulled me back.

The silk was so rotten with age that even the weak breeze tore it slightly, and I thought at the time that Vair's sharp 'Don't' was uttered because of the damage I had unwittingly done. It was a relic of treachery and bloodshed, but we both regarded it with a queer sort of reverence, as if it were associated with something sacred.

I should think an hour must have passed before we mentioned anything else. We were both agreed that one of us should write to a newspaper announcing our discovery and that the scarf should be cleaned by an expert and offered to a museum. One remark of Vair's struck me at the time as a little strange, but the full force of it did not come to me until some hours later.

'I wish you hadn't waved it out of the window,' he said. 'It's what that damned traitor did. That's what made you do it, of course—trying to re-enact part of an old tragedy.'

'I don't see that it matters,' I returned lightly. 'Nobody saw.'

He turned on me at once.

'How do you know?' he demanded sharply.

I could not help laughing then.

'My dear fellow,' I exclaimed, 'are you afraid that the wife or daughter of one of your neighbours will think '

'I wasn't thinking of them,' he returned curtly. 'When that rag was waved out of that window nearly three hundred years ago, you know what happened, you know what it brought into the house.'

I thought I had caught the drift of his meaning. Vair had always declined to walk under ladders or make the thirteenth of a party, and he was unhappy for days after he had spilled the contents of a salt-cellar.

'Oh, don't be an ass, Vair,' I begged. 'If there's any ill-luck about I give it leave to attack me and leave you alone.'

He did not answer, and in a few minutes the incident had passed temporarily from my mind.

I have tried to tell this story so many times by word of mouth, and been compelled at this point to pause and hesitate, as now I am compelled to pause and think. It is not that my memory fails me; memory, indeed, serves me all too well. But hereabouts I am brought to realize the failure of my small command of words. A bad speaker can at least convey something otherwise unexpressed by look, gesture, hesitation, tone of voice. But with nothing but pen, ink, paper, and a limited vocabulary, I see little chance of giving an adequate account of what happened to us that night, of how with the twilight depression was laid upon us, straw by straw, and how with the coming of darkness horror was laid upon us, load by load.

Even before supper I found myself restless and ill at ease. Something began to weigh upon my spirit as if my mind carried the knowledge of some ordeal which I had presently to face. Of course, I put it down to an attack of 'liver' and made up my mind to forget it. The intention was good, but it was unjustified by the desired result.

My discovery that Vair was suffering from a similar malaise did not help my own case. His spirits were far below normal, and I think our mutual discovery that the other was 'below form' added weight to that which was already dragging at our hearts. To make matters worse we each began to act for the other's benefit, to force laughter, to crack heavy jokes, and make cumbersome epigrams. But when at twilight we lit the lamp and sat down to supper we tacitly agreed to give up pretending.

'Do you feel that there's a weight crushing you whenever there's thunder about?' Vair asked suddenly.

I was glad to think of some excuse to account for my mood and answered quickly, 'Yes, very often. And I wouldn't mind betting there's some thunder about tonight.'

Vair looked at me and seemed suddenly to change his mind over what he had been about to say. He shook his head.

'The glass hasn't gone down.'

I rose from the table without apology, went to the window, pulled aside the curtains, and looked out. It was just after sunset on a very perfect May evening. There was a red glow in the west, and around this glow there was an area of sky which was almost apple-green. This merged into a very deep blue in which one or two pale stars were already beginning to play hide-and-seek.

'No,' I agreed grudgingly, 'there isn't a cloud in the sky. Still, storms come up very quickly.'

'Yes,' said Vair, 'and so do other things.'

My lips moved to ask him what he meant, but I thought better of it. Whatever morbid imaginings he might be entertaining, they were scarcely likely to help my own mood We ate in silence, continuing thus for a long time before I forced a laugh and exclaimed, 'Well, we're a jolly pair, aren't we? What the devil's the matter with us this evening? I only wish I knew.'

'I only wish I didn't think I know,' he answered strangely.

'Well, what do you think'

'I think we ought to go out somewhere tonight and stay out.'

'Why? You haven't felt like this before, have you?'

'No. And it's because I haven't felt like this before'

He came to another sudden pause, and we looked into each other's faces for a moment before he lowered his gaze.

'Now, look here,' I said, trying to keep my voice steady, 'let's be as honest as we can and try to analyse this thing. I'll say it first. We're both afraid of something. '

He went a step further.

'We're both afraid of the same thing,' he said.

'Well, what is it, then? Let's find out and confront it. When a horse shies at a tree you lead him up to it to show him that it's only a tree.'

'If it happens to be a tree or something like a tree. But if it isn't. . . Look here, let's go out. Straight away now, while there's time. They've got bedrooms at the Wellingford Arms. Let's go and spend the night there.'

With all my heart I wanted to go. But Pride borrowed the voice of Reason and spoke for me.

'Oh, don't let's make fools of ourselves,' I urged. 'I for one don't want to truckle to my nerves. If we give way like this once we shall always be doing it.'

He shrugged his shoulders.

'Let's have a drink.'

He brought out the whisky. I am a temperate man with a weak head for spirits, and I admit that I exceeded my usual allowance, but it made no more difference to me than if it were water. We sat facing each other gloomily in a silence which became increasingly difficult to break.

The unusual quality of this silence had already begun to impress me when Vair mentioned it, as if my thought had communicated itself to him. 'Don't you notice how extraordinarily still everything seems?' he asked presently.

'Yes,' I agreed, and snatched suddenly at a straw. 'The silence before the storm. There is a storm about, you see. '

He shook his head.

'No,' he said. 'It isn't that kind of stillness.'

And then, with a little leap of the heart and a tingling of the nostrils I suddenly realized a fact which seemed to me inexpressibly ugly. This stillness was not the hush of Nature before some electrical disturbance. For some time past we had heard no sound at all from the outer world. The gramophones and pianos in the little houses around us were all silent. It was the hour when at many houses on the estate hosts and guests were parting for the night, yet there was not the faint echo of a voice, nor the comfortable workaday sound of a car droning along a road. It may seem ludicrous, but I would have given a hundred pounds just then to hear the distant shunting of a train.

Vair rose suddenly, went to the window and looked out. I followed him.

For some while now it had been completely dark. Overhead in a very clear sky the stars looked peacefully into our troubled eyes.

'No storm about,' said Vair shortly.

He heard me catch my breath, and a moment later he was aware of what I had already perceived.

'Look! There aren't any lights! There isn't a light anywhere!'

It was true. The hour was not late, and yet from the rows of houses which began not so many yards distant, not a light was visible, nor was it possible to discern an outline of roof or chimney against the sky. We had been cut off from the lights and sounds of the outside world as completely as if we were in a cavern miles under the ground, save that our isolation—I can think of no other word—was lateral.

Vair's voice had risen high and thin. He made no effort to disguise the terror in it.

'There must be some fog about,' I said; and I was so anxious lest my voice should sound like Vair's that I spoke out of the base of my chest.

'Fog! Look, man!'

I looked. Truly there was not the least sign of fog or mist. Until we raised our eyes to the sky we stared into impenetrable, featureless darkness. Vair let the window curtains fall from his hand. He turned to me in the oppressive stillness, and his face worked until by an effort he controlled the muscles.

'Try to tell me,' he said hoarsely, 'what you've been feeling all evening.'

'How can I? The same as you, I suppose!' A reminiscence of soldiering came back to me. 'It's been like waiting to go over the top. A horrible aching anxiety. No, something more than that. A sense of being trapped, of being surrounded'

'Surrounded!' He caught up the word with a cry. 'That's just what you are! That's just what we both are!'

I drew him away from the curtained window.

'Surrounded! By what?' I made myself ask.

He spread out his hands and shook them helplessly.

'The Powers of Darkness, Hatred, Blood-lust, Intolerance—they were all waiting, waiting for the signal. Do you think these things die like spent matches? Do you think the black act of treachery', which brought them into this house, left nothing behind it. They were waiting—all these years—I tell you!' Suddenly he bared his teeth at me. 'You fool, to have waved that rag at them!'

Just for a moment I felt my brain turning like a wheel, but I made a fight for my sanity and won it back.

'Look here,' I said, 'for God's sake don't let's behave like madmen. Let's get out of it if the house is going to affect us like this.'

He stared back at me, giving me a look which I could not read.

'No,' he muttered; 'you wanted to stay.'

'Let's go down to the Wellingford Arms.'

'They're closed now.'

'It doesn't matter. They know you. They'll open for you.'

I found myself lusting for the world beyond that unnatural girdle of darkness. The Wellingford Arms, with its vulgar tin advertisements of Somebody's Beer, and Somebody Else's Whisky, and its framed Christmas Number plates—at least there was sanity there.

But Vair suddenly turned on me the eyes of a hunted animal.

'You fool!' he burst out. 'It's too late! We can't pass through *Them!*'

'What do you mean?' I faltered.

'They're all around us. You know it, too. They'll break in—in their own good time—as they did before. We're trapped, I tell you!'

Against my will, and Heaven knows how hard I fought for disbelief, Vair had captured my powers of reason. In theory, if not in action, I was now prepared to follow him like a child.

'What do they want?' I stammered.

'Us! One of us or both! What did Murder and Hatred and Blood-lust ever want but sacrifice?'

He fairly spat the words at me and I seized his arm.

'Come on,' I said, 'we're going to get out of this. We're going to run the gauntlet.'

'Ah,' said Vair thickly. 'If we can.'

We must have crossed the hall, although I do not remember it. My next recollection is of helping Vair in his fumbling with the bolts and lock of the great door. We wrenched it open and stood looking at an opaque wall of darkness.

I tried to force myself across the threshold, only to find myself standing rigid. As in a nightmare, my legs were shackled so that I could not move a step forward, but although terror clawed at me like a wild beast, my senses were keenly and even painfully alert.

I knew that this belt of darkness around the house was alive with whisperings and movements, with all manner of stealthiness, which lurked only just beyond the horizon of vision and the limits of hearing. And as I stood straining eyes and ears I knew that the barriers must soon break and that I should both see and hear.

We stood thus a long while on the edge of the threshold we could not pass, but whether it were seconds or minutes I could not say. To us it seemed hours ere the darkness passed, melting into the living forms of men. We could see, and there was movement everywhere; we could hear, and voices were shouting orders, although the actual words eluded us. They were human voices with strange nasal intonations, snarling and shouting. Even in my extremity I remembered having heard that the soldiery of Cromwell had affected a hideous nasal accent. And now the darkness was sundered and shivered by a score of lights, the lights of naked torches which nodded to the rhythm of men marching. I saw the glint of them on the metal heads of pikes, and on the long barrels of muskets outlined clearly now against a naked sky of stars.

Terror may bind a man to the spot, but another turn of the rack may torture him back into motion. So it was with us. Blind instinct alone made me slam the great door and shoot the nearest heavy bolt. I saw Vair groping for me like a tear-blinded child and I took his arm. We ran futilely back into the room we had vacated and crouched in the corner farthest from the door, while great noises like thunder began to reverberate through the house, as pike-handles and musket-butts crashed sickeningly on the great outer door.

We must both have taken leave of reason then, for neither Vair nor I can remember anything more until the great nail-studded door, smashed off its hinges, fell on to the broken flags of the hall with the loudest crash of all. The tramp of feet, mingled with the sound of arms carelessly handled, thudding against floor and wall, and with the sharp nasal snarling of voices. In a moment it seemed they were everywhere—in the hall, on the main staircase, in the room over our heads.

Vair had all this time the grip of a madman on my wrist, and suddenly he leaned to me and screamed into my ear, 'The Chapel . . . under the roof. . . it's consecrated . . . there's a chance . . . there's a chance, I tell you . . . '

'They're on the stairs' I cried back in my despair.

'The back stairs! Come on!'

A second door in the old room gave access to a passage leading to the back stairs. Those stairs we knew to be unsafe, but ordinary human peril was something far beyond and beneath our consideration. I remember the rumble and murmur of sounds about the house as we rushed out into the passage. Footfalls and voices sounded everywhere, and musket-butts were smiting heavily against stairs and walls. As we stumbled and ran I expected at every step to be seized and overwhelmed by some horrible and nameless Power.

How we reached the attics I cannot now say. The narrow, crumbling staircase creaked and swayed under us, and once I went down thigh deep through a rotten stair, with splinters of hard wood tearing clothes and flesh. But we were near the top ere the hunt had scented their game and sounds of pursuit began to clamour behind us.

Vair forced open the door of the little room which had once been a chapel. I blundered in over his body, which lay prone just across the threshold. He had fallen unconscious, and I had to force his legs aside before I could close the door. I slammed it to in the faces of vague forms which filled the passage to the stair-head, and drove home the wooden bolt inside.

And then it seemed to me that our pursuers recoiled from that closed door like a great wave from the base of a cliff, and ugly cries outside died down to uneasy whisperings, and instinctively I knew that we were safe. I must have fainted then, for I remember nothing more until I woke in bright sunlight. Vair was sitting beside me, watching me, with a chalk-like face. We hardly spoke, but sought each other's hands like frightened children.

Eventually we nerved ourselves to go downstairs into the ruin and disorder of the old house, through which, one might have thought, a whirlwind had passed during the night.

A.M. Burrage – The Life And Times.

Alfred McLelland Burrage, better known as simply AM Burrage, was born in Hillingdon, Middlesex on July 1st, 1889, to Alfred Sherrington Burrage and Mary E. Burrage. On his Father's side writing already ran in the family's blood as both he and an uncle, Edwin Harcourt Burrage, were writers of the then very popular boys' magazine fiction.

Life in late Victorian times was by no means easy and writing has always been a precarious career for most. For an insight into the young AM and his surroundings it is interesting to see how certain facts were captured in the 1891 census when he was aged one. The family is listed as living at Uxbridge Common in Hillingdon. His father is 40 and his mother 36. In the next census of 1901, and with it the end of the Victorian era, the family has moved to 1 Park Villa, Newbury. In that time his father has aged 17 years his mother 6 years and young AM has disappeared from the records. It's almost a precursor to one of his stories.

There is little documented about his growing up and education. What we can glean though is something about his environment. His neighbours were varied: a tailor's journeyman, a corn porter, a lodging-house keeper and a grocer's assistant. Nothing particularly illustrious, so times cannot have been as rosy as they should, especially in the light of his Father's hard work. Alfred Sherrington wrote for The Boy's World, Our Boys' Paper, The Boys of England, and various others. He also appears to have written under the pseudonym Philander Jackson and edited The Boys' Standard and that one of his more celebrated pieces was a retelling of the story of Sweeney Todd entitled "The String of Peals; or, Passages from the Life of Sweeney Todd, the Demon Barber".

Sadly Alfred Sherrington Burrage died in 1906. There is a biographical note in Lloyd's Magazine, from 1921, which suggests that young Alfred McLelland was studying at St. Augustine's, the Catholic Foundation School in Ramsgate, and most probably away from home at the time.

A.M. Burrage was 16 years old when he had his first story published; the same year as his father's death, in the prestigious boys' paper, Chums. It was a great start to his professional career and whether doors had been opened by his father and family or not the young man's career now had to stand on its own. He was now primary provider for the household and this was the only way he could do it. His Mother, sister and aunt must be provided for.

Magazine fiction was his family's blood and business and for A. M. Burrage, business was good. He established himself as a competent and creative writer and was busy writing stories and articles on a weekly basis for publications such as Boys' Friend Weekly, Boys' Herald, Comic Life, Vanguard, Dreadnought, Triumph Library Cheer Boys Cheer, and Gem, under the pseudonym 'Cooee'.

However, unlike his father and uncle who had remained firmly and easily categorised as boys' writers, he had his sights set on the more well regarded, more lucrative, adult market. Burrage was aided in his early years as a professional writer by Isobel Thorne of the off-Fleet Street publishing firm Shurey's. Her publications have been characterised as "low in price, modest in payments, but whose readers were avid for romance, thrills, sensation, strong characterisation and neat plotting", and this estimation of her publications also fits nicely the description of Burrage's own writing at that time. For a young writer this sort of readership was vital, and the modest wages he received were bolstered by the exposure the publications brought him. Burrage was certainly helped by Thorne's use of young writers.

At the time Burrage was beginning to really establish himself as a writer, the entire magazine fiction scene was benefiting from what we would now see as disruptive influences: new printing techniques, a growing readership with more disposable income and leisure time and other media failing to provide – though obviously movies and such were only in their infancy at the time. The market was lively and commercial, and the readership interested, excitable and willing to pay. P. G. Wodehouse, of Jeeves fame, recalls these years:

We might get turned down by the Strand, but there was always the hope of landing with Nash's, the Story-teller, the London, the Royal, the Red, the Yellow, Cassell's, the New, the Novel, the Grand, the Pall Mall, and the Windsor, not to mention Blackwood's, Cornhill, Chambers's and probably about a dozen more I've forgotten.

With War clouds darkening the skies of Europe in 1914 Burrage was firmly established as a magazine writer, securing publication in London Magazine and The Storyteller, which were both highly prestigious publications. Alongside he had plenty printed in less illustrious publications such as Short Stories Illustrated.

By now Burrage, a young man of twenty-four-year-was eligible for the Armed Services. Under the 'Derby Scheme' he confirmed that he was available for service if called upon in December 1915. Conscription was to follow shortly though, by that time, Burrage had already voluntarily enrolled in the Artists Rifles.

The significance of Burrage's decision to join the Artists Rifles is made clear by the nature of the unit itself. They formed in the middle of the nineteenth century, a group of volunteer artists comprising musicians, writers, painters and engravers. Minerva and Mars were their patrons, one of wisdom, arts, and defence, the other of war. The unit boasted several significant figures as ex-servicemen, including Dante Gabriel Rossetti, Algernon Charles Swinburne and William Morris. It was a popular unit with students and recent postgraduates, and the training was considered and extensive.

In Burrage's vivid, celebrated account of World War I entitled War is War, he insists that he was a volunteer and not a conscript, though as has already been noted, it is quite possible that his decision to join such a respected territorial unit may have been more of an effort to secure himself a more congenial army posting; had he waited for conscription, he would have had little choice over those with whom he was posted. Unlike poets Wilfred Owen or Edward Thomas, Burrage did not achieve a commission, and he suggests in War is War that this may be a result of his extremely unmilitary personality and his shortcomings as a soldier.

Add to this the fact that as the breadwinner for the family he was putting himself in harm's way. If anything were to happen to him the result on the family would be devastating. With the death of
Edwin Harcourt Burrage in 1916 it came even more starkly into focus.

Even though he was now a soldier he was still a writer and writers had to write. It also helped that it was a distraction from the mindless carnage around him. He experimented with various genres, excelling in the one that was to prove most lucrative for him; the light romance, in which a male character invariably meets a female character, there is a problem or hurdle to their being together, they overcome it and they live happily ever after. Burrage's talent for this formula was such that he could work seemingly endless minor variations from the same basic storyline and so he was able to keep writing a steady body of easy work.

He gives a fascinating account of the practicalities of writing such fiction during wartime in War is War, in which he remarks on the difficulties of censorship: "the problem of censorship was an acute one to me. It was well enough to write a story, but the difficulty was to get it censored. Officers were shy of tackling five thousand words or so, written in indelible pencil..." After some time he managed to find a chaplain who was willing to undertake the censorship. However, in order to secure this chaplain's favour and thus his services he was obliged to appear to be holy. Though he did so in earnest while he was with the chaplain, his efforts were dashed when the chaplain found him, sprawled on top of a young girl, and realised Burrage's piety to be a fraudulent con. As Burrage had anticipated, the reality of his behaviour ensured that this particular opportunity was swiftly ended. Resourceful to the last, though, he writes of his solution: "there were 'green envelopes' which could be sent away sealed and were liable only to censorship at the base, but these were only sparingly issued... I met an A.S.C. lorry driver who had stolen enough green envelopes to last me for the rest of the war; and since he only wanted two francs for them I was free of the censorship from that day forward."

Although we know that Burrage had his family to support at home as an incentive to keep writing, at times in War is War he reveals a more intimate aspect of his relationship with his work.

"It was a great relief to me to write when it was at all possible – to sit down and lose myself in that pleasant old world I used to know and pretend to myself that there never had been a war. Some of my editors seemed of the opinion that we were not suffering from one now. One used to write to me saying "Couldn't you let me have one of your light, charming love stories of country house life by next Thursday." I would get these letters in the trenches during the usual 'morning hate' when my fingers were too numb to hold a pencil, when I was worn out with work and sleeplessness, and when I was extremely doubtful if there ever would be another Thursday".

Writing is a useful therapy and for Burrage it provided a means to escape if only for a short time to a world that he could control and move at will. With the misery and harsh conditions of the War dragging on he was eventually invalided and so he returned to England.

One of the best insights we have as to the character which Burrage presented on his return from the war is to be found in Lloyd's's 1920 publication of Captain Dorry, one of Burrage's story series. In that publication there was included a brief sketch of Burrage, describing his personality.

A.M. BURRAGE is the type of young man who might very well walk out of one of his own stories. He commenced yarn-spinning as a boy of fifteen at St Augustine's, Ramsgate, writing stories of school life to provide himself with pocket-money. Since then he has won his spurs as one of the most popular of magazine writers. Everything he does has charm and reflects his own romantic spirit – for he is incurably romantic and hopelessly lazy. It is his misfortune, although he would not admit it, that his work finds a too ready market. Nevertheless, his friends hope that one day he will wake up and do justice to himself. Otherwise he may end up as a "best-seller", a fate which doubtless he contemplates with equanimity.

Despite the sketch's fairly accurate but negative summation of Burrage's literary output up to that point, some of his stories seem to exhibit a desire to write about more than just his usual romantic plots. The most immediate change of this nature is in his decision to bring some of his wartime experience into his work, despite being perfectly aware that such writing was not at all what his editors desired, for they feared it would upset and intimidate their readership.

An example of this can be found in "A Town of Memories", published in 1919 in Grand Magazine, in which he uses his well rehearsed romantic story with a slight shift of emphasis to explore his own return from the war and the general reception which soldiers received on their return. Following a young officer as he returns to the town in which he grew up, Burrage portrays an almost hostile environment into which he returns; he is unrecognised, and nobody pays any interest, respect or attention to him or his stories of the war, nor even to his reception of the Distinguished Service Order. Instead, the people of the town have their own interests and priorities with which to concern themselves. Though this contentious portrayal of post-war society certainly marks a slight shift in Burrage's writing, he returns to the romantic convention expected of him by reuniting the officer with a beautiful girl who had admired him throughout school. It would be harsh to not accept that market conditions expected one thing and to ignore them would mean turning his back on publications who still clamoured for his penmanship.

Another of Burrage's alternative directions is to be found in "The Recurring Tragedy", in which a General whose war tactics of attrition had been to the slaughtered cost of his soldiers, and he comes to re-imagine his own past as a Judas figure in a terrible vision. The Strange Career of Captain Dorry became a series for Lloyd's Magazine in 1920 about a gentleman crook and an ex-officer with a Military Cross who, idle in peacetime, meets a mysterious man called Fewgin whose business is in stolen goods and mind reading. Fewgin realises Dorry is a suitable candidate for recruitment into his gang of like-minded ex-military thieves, stealing only from "certain vampires who made money out of the war, and, by keeping up prices, are continuing to make money out of the peace". Again, in this motive, we see a glimpse of Burrage's own feelings on the war, as there is undoubtedly a bitterness towards those profiting from the suffering of others in such a manner. Fewgin justifies himself, saying:

"I help brave men who cannot help themselves. I give them a chance to get back a little of their own from the men who battened and fattened on them, who helped to starve their dependents while they were fighting, who smoked fat cigars in the haunts of their betters, and hoped the war might never end."

Burrage began to see slightly more success in the 1920s, achieving a couple of hard back publications entitled Some Ghost Stories and Poor Dear Esme. The latter, a comedy, concerns a boy who, for various reasons, is forced to disguise himself as a girl. Though these hard cover publications were a notable achievement, and one of which he was proud, the fact was that there was less money in it than in the magazines. In his history of the Strand Magazine, Reginald Pound portrays Burrage around this time, likening him to his equally prolific contemporary Herbert Shaw, considering them "two Bohemian temperaments that suffused and at times confused gifts from which more was expected than come forth. They had a precise knowledge of the popular short story as the product of calculated design. Both privately despised it, though it was their living."

The early 1920s, and with them a boom in prosperity, hope and happiness, now brought with them an increase in demand for war stories. Rather than preferring to ignore the atrocities of the war, which had seemed the general attitude in the immediate post-war years, society became more interested and concerned with the manner in which the war was fought, and the greed and political battles which had necessitated such bloodshed. Burrage answered this demand in 1930 with his own epochal piece, War Is War. He published under the pseudonym 'Ex-Private X', saying "were it otherwise I could not tell the truth about myself", though its publisher, Victor Gollancz, "who published the book and greatly admired it, had to point out that the critics would hardly take the book seriously if it became known that the author earned his living producing two or three slushy love stories a week".

In one of a series of letters he wrote to his contemporary and fellow writer Dorothy Sayers, Burrage bemoans how War is War "promised to be a great success, but was only a moderate one". The book itself was received with reviews on both sides of the spectrum. Cyril Fall's War Books, a survey of post-war writing published in 1930, gives a clear indication as to why the critics were so mixed in reception of the book. He writes:

This book is extremely uneven in quality. The account of the attack at Paschendaele and of conditions at Cambrai after the great German counter-attack are very good indeed; in fact among the best of their kind. But the rest is disfigured by an unreasoned and unpleasant attack on superiors and all troops other than those of the front line, which is all the more astonishing because the author is inclined to harp upon his social position as compared with that of many of the officers with whom he came in contact. He does not use as much bad language as many writers on the War, but his methods of abuse will leave on some of his readers at least a worse impression than the most highly-spiced language.

Dorothy Sayers was the editor at Victor Gollanz for anthologies of ghost and horror stories which included stories by Burrage. She says, in one of her letters of Burrage's story The Waxwork, a piece beyond the nerves of the editors, "what you say about "The Waxwork" sounds very exciting, just the sort of thing I want. Our nerves are stronger than those of the editors of periodicals, and we will publish anything, so long as it does not bring us into conflict with the Home Secretary". Though their correspondence began as strictly business, Burrage's acquaintance with Atherton Fleming, Sayers's husband, allowed their interactions to become less formal and friendlier. Burrage wrote of Fleming "I hope to encounter him soon in one of the Fleet Street tea-shops". 'Tea-shop' being a popular euphemism for the pub, where both Burrage and Fleming could frequently be found, though their alcohol consumption came to damage both their health and their professions, with Burrage coming off the worse.

Happily for Burrage, as a result of being featured in one of Sayers's anthologies, The Waxwork became one of his best-known stories and it would grab the attention of the film companies several times down the years even becoming an episode in the TV series 'Alfred Hitchcock Presents'.

The developing friendship between Burrage and Sayers enabled him to reveal more details of his personal life, admitting to her his "neuritis at both ends (legs and eyes)", and hinting at his troubles with alcohol: "Fleet Street is not a good place for a man who delights in succumbing to temptation, and whose doctor says that even small doses of alcohol are poison to him". Sayers sympathises, replying that Fleming "agrees with you entirely about the temptations of Fleet Street; he has, however, succeeded, through sheer strength of character, in being able to drink soda-water in the face of all his fellow journalists".

In another of Burrage's letters, he apologises for a delay in sending proofs of a story, with the words:

I have had a pretty thin time lately through illness and anxiety. And for days on end haven't had the energy in me to write a letter, and when I had the energy to send a complete set of proofs to you I found I hadn't the postage money (This is when you take out your handkerchief and start sobbing). I owed my late agent over £1000, so I got practically nothing out of War is War. He stuck to it. Well, he is paid off now, and so are my arrears of income tax. All this took a toll of my very small earning capacity, and I have been sold up. This on top of something which promised to be a great success and was only a moderate one, was a bit too much for me. Still, in spite of sickness I am resilient and shall float again. "You can't keep a good man down," as the whale said about Jonah.

For a man who had so many stories in so many magazines, and was gaining pace in Sayers's anthologies as a talented writer of horror stories, his income will have been far higher than the then average wage, and yet as he says, he finds himself short of money.

Several questions are left unanswered about his personal life. It is unclear whether he was still supporting family, or whether he spent the majority of his money on alcohol, or whether he chose to conceal his true fortunes from those around him. Perhaps most incongruous is the apparent absence of a wife; though his death certificate indicates that he had one, listed as H.A. Burrage, he seems never to mention her to Sayers.

He was around forty-two when he wrote that apology letter to Sayers, though in tone and circumstance it seems to be from a man in a far later stage of his life.

Burrage continued writing until his death in 1956, and continued to be prolifically published. Indeed, the Evening News alone published some forty of his stories between 1950-56. His death is recorded at Edgware General Hospital on 18th December, and the causes of his death are recorded as congestive cardiac failure, arteriosclerosis and chronic bronchitis. He was sixty-seven years old, and his last address is listed as 105 Vaughan Road, Harrow.

Though his name is not often remembered in lists of prominent writers of his time, or even it's genres, his ghost stories are highly regarded by critics and fans alike, while his life story tells us much about the trials and stresses placed on authors during and after the war, and on soldiers returning from that war. His reluctant acceptance that the money was in the magazines while the esteem was in the poorly-paying hard covers, and his persistence as a writer, speak of a determined man, doomed to circumstance yet living as best he could.

In ending A.M Burrage wrote a few sentences which best sum up two things. Firstly his love for his son Simon (who sadly passed away in October 2013 and was a great and passionate advocate for his Father's works.) and secondly his succinct reasons for writing.

TO JULIAN SIMON FIELD BURRAGE
who at the moment of writing will
soon achieve the great age of four.
From somebody who loves him.

In War is War I admitted being a professional writer, or in other words one who depends for his bread and cheese and beer on writing, typing or dictating strings of sentences which his masters, the Public, are kind enough to buy and presumably to read.

The book brought me letters from a few old friends and a great many new ones. A large percentage of the new friends, who missed having seen that my identity was rather unkindly betrayed by the Press, wrote and asked (a) who I was and (b) what sort of stories did I write?

The answer to the second question will be found in the following pages. The answer to the first question is 'Nobody Much', worse luck.

Most of these stories were written with the intention of giving the reader a pleasant shudder, in the hope that he will take a lighted candle to bed with him—for candle-makers must be considered in these hard times. Some have already made their bow from the pages of the monthly magazines. The best have, quite naturally, been rejected.

www.ingramcontent.com/pod-product-compliance
Lightning Source LLC
Chambersburg PA
CBHW060132260626
47160CB00005B/2081